"I'm worried about you, Em. Is that such a crime?"

Never had Drew encountered such an exasperating, stubborn, sinfully sensual woman. His conscience told him to walk away now and keep going until he'd gained enough distance so he couldn't look back.

What was it about this particular woman? Why, out of all the women he'd dated—and there'd been plenty—was she the one to make him forget his cardinal rule of absolutely no involvement?

Emily's eyes darkened, the color reminding him of thunderclouds at midnight. Wild. Untamable. Worthy of a power he deeply respected. A hypnotic, sensual power she effortlessly and unconsciously wielded over him in ways he'd never imagined possible.

He dipped his head, but stopped before his lips brushed against hers. Her warm breath caressed his mouth.

"This is a mistake," she whispered.

He waited for her to push him away. She didn't.

"What's life without a few mistakes along the way?"

She grinned, and her soft laughter made him smile. "Pretty darned boring."

Dear Reader,

Have you ever had one of those days when just about everything goes wrong? No matter where you go or what you do, it seems as if a black cloud is following you?

Emily Dugan is having one of *those* days. In twenty-four hours her life is turned upside down by a series of events that would leave most of us struggling to catch our breath. So when she literally falls at the feet of scrumptious arson inspector Drew, the youngest of the three ultrasexy Perry brothers in my SOME LIKE IT HOT trilogy, she's certain things have just gone from bad to...better?

Commitment-shy Drew is always game for a short-term relationship, and the hotter the better. But when sassy, seductive Emily keeps turning up the heat to rival the heat wave blanketing the city, even he has a hard time keeping his cool.

I hope you enjoy Drew and Emily's steamy romance. And be sure to join me next month for *Under Fire* (Temptation #950), the final story in the SOME LIKE IT HOT trilogy. Until then...

Warmest regards,

Jamie Denton

Books by Jamie Denton

HARLEQUIN TEMPTATION
708—FLIRTING WITH DANGER
748—THE SEDUCTION OF SYDNEY
767—VALENTINE FANTASY
793—RULES OF ENGAGEMENT
797—BREAKING THE RULES
857—UNDER THE COVERS
942—SLOW BURN*

HARLEQUIN BLAZE
10—SLEEPING WITH
   THE ENEMY
41—SEDUCED BY
   THE ENEMY

* Some Like It Hot

Jamie Denton
HEATWAVE

HARLEQUIN®

TORONTO • NEW YORK • LONDON
AMSTERDAM • PARIS • SYDNEY • HAMBURG
STOCKHOLM • ATHENS • TOKYO • MILAN • MADRID
PRAGUE • WARSAW • BUDAPEST • AUCKLAND

For Stephanie

ISBN 0-373-69146-7

HEATWAVE

Copyright © 2003 by Jamie Ann Denton.

This edition published by arrangement with Harlequin Books S.A.

® and TM are trademarks of the publisher. Trademarks indicated with
® are registered in the United States Patent and Trademark Office, the
Canadian Trade Marks Office and in other countries.

Visit us at www.eHarlequin.com

Printed in U.S.A.

1

As far as Emily Dugan was concerned, New York City had the only decent cab drivers in the country. Case in point, the rude excuse for a cabbie who'd left her and her bags at the curb in front of the Norris Culinary Academy on the hottest day to hit Southern California in over a decade. Even at four in the afternoon, not so much as a whisper of an ocean breeze ruffled the palm trees high overhead, or dared to hint at the promise of relief from the blistering heatwave.

The thickening afternoon traffic on Santa Monica Boulevard whizzed past her as she fought back another wave of nausea. The last thing she wanted during her much-needed month-long vacation was another bout of the flu that had plagued her weeks ago, which had followed on the heels of the most wicked cold she'd ever suffered. She'd been looking forward to this visit with her grandmother for over a month. Nothing, she thought determinedly, not the flu or even the mess her life had unexpectedly become, was going to put a damper on a visit with Grandy. Besides, she had some big decisions to make. The relative peace and quiet would provide her ample opportunity to take the steps necessary to set her life back on track.

She pulled in a deep breath and let it out slowly in an

effort to quell another bout of nausea. Tugging up the handle on the largest suitcase, she piggybacked the matching smaller case, then slung her carry-on over her shoulder. An acrid scent filled the air, like wood smoke or maybe burning charcoal from a neighbor's backyard barbecue, only nowhere near as pleasant.

Since the parking lot to the right of the building was vacant this late in the afternoon, Emily avoided the front entrance of the cooking school her grandmother had started nearly fifty years ago, and wheeled her luggage along the side to the house in back where Grandy still lived. The sight of chipped stucco and peeling paint on the side of the school building took her a little by surprise, as did the thin wisps of grass growing between the cracks in the concrete path. The Norris Culinary Academy had always been Grandy's pride and joy, and for as long as Emily could remember, had been kept in nothing but pristine condition.

She reached the wooden gate and pulled the handle with her free hand. The hinges creaked, as if unaccustomed to movement. Dragging her luggage behind her, she pushed through the gate and stepped into the courtyard. She frowned as she did a quick glance around the area. The acrid scent of burnt...something, assaulted her. The wonderland where she'd played as a child retained a mere shadow of its former beauty.

Small patches of dark moss dotted the putti fountain in the courtyard's center, while the small pond below stood bone-dry. Weeds choked the flower beds running along the front of the house. Even the large white plastic urns, usually filled to overflowing with petunias, portulaca or begonias, housed nothing more than the shriveled remains of their original inhabitants.

Something was definitely wrong, but when she'd spoken to Grandy on the phone two days ago to reconfirm their plans, everything had appeared to be the same as always. Never had Emily expected to find the property in such a state of neglect.

She maneuvered her luggage up the two brick steps of the porch to the house and knocked on the door. The only sound came from the distant traffic on the boulevard behind her, and the gentle hum from the central air conditioning unit one of her uncles had installed for Grandy a couple of years ago. Emily didn't hear a sound from the television or one of her grandmother's Big-Band-era CDs, which Grandy often played while puttering around her house. Absolute silence.

Perhaps she'd gone out for the afternoon, but that, too, was highly unlikely. Her grandmother, a creature of habit, reserved errands and shopping for Saturday mornings. Emily decided to check the garage first, then she'd unearth the key hidden on the porch and let herself inside to wait.

She parked her luggage in the shade of the porch, then turned and found herself looking into the most stunning pair of sea-green eyes this side of heaven. Alarm skidded down her spine. She'd been so absorbed in her concern, she hadn't even heard anyone behind her, something a New Yorker *never* did. She must be more upset by the recent and completely unexpected turn of events in her life than she realized.

"Can I help you?" she asked cautiously. She took a

good look at him, committing his features to memory.
With her luck lately, anything was possible and she
wanted to be able to give the police an accurate description. She might forget the way his eyes skimmed
her body, and she could have a hard time remembering her name, but she doubted she wouldn't remember
how his angular features seemed carved from granite.
Too bad he wore a frown that would make Ebenezer
Scrooge proud, she thought, because with this man's
chiseled good looks and his slightly wavy hair the
color of rich mink, he'd be nothing short of scrumptious if he actually smiled. Not that it mattered to her.
She was through with men.

"I was about to ask you the same thing." He had one
of those deep, smooth voices capable of coaxing a
woman to do just about anything. Oh, she knew the
type well. A charmer, and incredibly dangerous to
women who made a habit of picking the wrong men.
Not that she would ever fall for something so blatantly
obvious again.

She smoothed her suddenly clammy palms down
the skirt of her loose floral summer dress. "I asked you
first." Okay, could she sound any more childish?

"I'm here on official business. And you are?"

Official business? He wasn't a cop. Cops didn't carry
shovels around with them. He did wear a badge,
though, and a crisp blue uniform that outlined a body
spectacular enough for a blue-jeans ad campaign. The
man was one-hundred-percent enticing. Well, maybe if
she was interested she might call him that, only she
wasn't. Much.

No, she firmly reminded herself. Men were a thing of the past for her. She was just too good at making the wrong decisions when it came to the opposite sex.

"What official business?"

He ignored her question. "Are you related to Mrs. Norris?"

"Yes," she said carefully. Her roiling stomach took another dip and swirl before settling back down. Feeling none too steady, she reached for the porch railing. "I'm her granddaughter."

He finally smiled and her breath deserted her. *Scrumptious* only scratched the surface. The laugh lines surrounding his eyes deepened, which told her that despite that earlier frown, this gorgeous man actually did smile, and often. "Then you must be Emily."

Obviously, he knew something she didn't, which made her feel a half step behind him in their conversation. When her stomach gave another lurch, she tightened her grip on the railing. "Who *are* you, and where is my grandmother?"

His smile widened. Was it really possible for this man to appear any more sinfully handsome?

Apparently so. Her pulse revved up, underscoring that very point.

He leaned his shovel against the porch before he moved up the steps. "Drew Perry," he said, extending his hand in greeting. "And your grandmother is going to be just fine."

That half step behind shifted into two giant steps as her vision went all funky and blurry on her for the space of two heartbeats. She shook her head to clear it. "*Going* to be fine? What happened? Where is she?"

"Hey, are you all right?" Drew asked. "You look pale."

"I'm fine." Except she didn't feel fine. Her voice sounded distant and tinny, a perfect accompaniment for the dull ringing in her ears. Either she was about to suffer a recurrence of the flu or the cardboard excuse for chicken cordon bleu she'd been served on the airplane planned to make an unwelcome reappearance.

She swayed slightly. "Just tell me what happened to my grandmother."

Warm, work-roughened hands settled over her bare arms as he gently urged her away from the railing to the brick steps. "Maybe you'd better sit down," he suggested.

Feeling decidedly fuzzy and tingly all at the same time, Emily didn't argue. She allowed him to assist her down onto the steps. Though she wasn't exactly certain what she expected to happen next, Drew taking her pulse didn't even make her list of possibilities. The feel of his fingers holding her wrist sent a chill down her spine and she shivered. A ridiculous reaction, especially considering the record hot temperatures.

"Your pulse always this high?" he asked her.

She tugged her hand away from him. "No," she lied. "It's not high, either."

The look he gave her said he knew otherwise. "Your pulse is elevated, and you're as pale as a sheet."

"The airline food didn't agree with me," she managed to say around another wave of nausea. "Will you please tell me who you are and what you've done with my grandmother?"

"I'm with the Los Angeles Fire Department. Your grandmother had a little accident and was transported by the paramedics to the emergency room."

Her stomach dipped and swirled again. "What kind of accident?"

He smiled again, causing her pulse to click up a couple more notches. "She's going to be fine," he said.

Why wouldn't he give her a straight answer? She shook her head again. Too late, she realized the drastic error in judgment. Her vision blurred and the ringing in her ears amplified.

"Emily? Stay with me, Emily."

She tried to tell him she wasn't going anywhere until he told her exactly what was going on, but her peripheral vision faded to gray. In a matter of seconds, all she could see was a minute pinpoint of light, filled with the rapidly disappearing vision of the handsome stranger, until the lights finally dimmed.

DREW HAD BECOME an arson inspector for a reason—he absolutely detested hospitals. In his opinion, emergency rooms were the worst. But here he was, at the UCLA Medical Center for the second time in one day, hanging around a place he didn't like, keeping a promise to an old woman he didn't even know. A sweet old woman who could very well be an arson suspect.

He leaned against the wall nearest the electronic doors a few feet away from the ER's waiting area. The space was crowded for a Thursday afternoon, with people hoping to be seen soon or anxious for word on the status of a loved one. A pair of sunshine-blond little boys played with plastic trucks on the asphalt-tile floor near the feet of a man Drew assumed was their father. The kids made car engine sounds and scooted their toys around in circles, seemingly oblivious to the worried expression on their father's face, or the fear and despair mingled in the guy's eyes.

Drew looked away as an old memory nudged him. He'd seen that look before, on his own dad's face as the family had waited to hear if his mother was going to pull through. But Drew had known. He might have only been a little squirt at the time, but he'd known that he and his older brothers would never see their mother again. The score of firefighters that had hovered around the emergency room that night pretty much told a story that even Drew, at the tender age of six, had known would not hold a happy ending. As an adult, twenty-three years later, he understood that Joanna Perry had died doing what she loved, fighting fires and saving lives. As a kid, he hadn't been quite so wise or understanding.

Like his oldest brother Ben, Drew had done his best to avoid doctors and hospitals ever since. As third-generation firefighters, they found visits to emergency rooms came with the job, but at least were somewhat minimal. Their brother, Cale, however, worked as a paramedic and passed through the electronic doors of the ER numerous times during each pull of duty. Since transferring to arson two years ago, Drew's trips here were slim to none unless he needed to question a witness with regard to an arson investigation. He couldn't avoid the sterile, antiseptic halls completely, but any time spent in hospitals now was routinely confined to the morgue or the medical examiner's office.

"Hey, what are you doing here? Come to ask that new ER nurse out on a date?"

Drew looked up and acknowledged his brother. "Cale," he said, straightening. "Speak of the devil."

"And the devil appears," Cale countered with a wide grin, something he'd been doing a lot of lately. Drew gave all the credit to Cale's fiancée, Maggie. Or was it Amanda? Amanda, he corrected. Maggie had been her persona when she'd been suffering amnesia. He really liked Amanda, but it had been a lot of fun to watch Maggie keeping his brother on his toes.

"So why are you hangin' around this place?" Cale asked. "Don't you have a firebug to catch?"

Drew let out a sigh. How exactly *did* he explain his presence in the ER, especially when he wasn't really sure himself how he came to be playing the role of knight in shining armor, not once, but twice in the same day? "Long story," he said, hoping Cale would leave it alone, because he had no easy answers.

Earlier today he'd come to the ER to question Velma Norris, the eighty-year-old owner of the Norris Culinary Academy, regarding the outbreak of recent fires at the school. While the fires themselves were relatively harmless in nature, Drew had his suspicions. First, a grease fire inside a deserted classroom, seemingly caused by a grease spill and a faulty pilot light. Then, a short tower of crates filled with newspapers behind the school had caught fire, caused, at first glance, by a careless smoker. The most recent incident—involving a Dumpster—had also looked innocuous on the surface, except the fire had been the third in two weeks. With the blazes occurring so close together, Drew didn't plan on dismissing the last case as accidental without proof.

To complicate matters, he'd never expected to be cajoled by Velma into returning to the school to meet her granddaughter, Emily, and bring her to the hospital. When Emily had literally fainted at his feet, he'd had no other choice but to bring her to the ER. With the record high temperatures, dehydration or heatstroke were real possibilities, and he didn't believe in taking chances.

Cale stuffed his hands in the front pockets of his navy uniform trousers. "Give me the condensed version. I've got a couple minutes until Brady finishes up."

Just his luck, Cale wouldn't be going anywhere anytime soon because his partner was damned thorough when it came to paperwork. "Someone passed out, and I was handy." Drew opted for a minimal exchange of information. "Heat exhaustion, I think."

Cale's grin widened. "A woman someone, no doubt."

Drew frowned. "Yeah, so?" He knew he had a reputation within the department as a ladies' man, however unfounded in his opinion, but it wasn't like that this time. He'd been doing someone a favor, and well, when a woman fainted at his feet, his training took over. Period. End of story. So what if he'd liked the way Emily Dugan's big brown eyes sparkled when she'd looked at him? Was it a crime for him to appreciate a beautiful woman?

Cale's laughter irritated Drew. "Only you, little brother, only you."

Usually the ribbing he received from his brothers or the guys at Trinity Station failed to get a rise out of him. Unfortunately, today was a different story. "What's that supposed to mean?"

"It means that you don't have enough women chasing after you, now you've got them falling at your feet."

"It wasn't like that."

"Really?" Cale crossed his arms, his expression skeptical. "Then how was it? It's not like you to wait around a hospital to find out about a patient."

"Like I said, it's a long story." One he didn't care to share with his brother at the moment, not when he had a hard time explaining his actions to himself.

"An interesting one, too, I'll bet." Cale sobered. "What's her name?"

Drew let out a sigh. "Emily Dugan, not that it's any of your business."

"She was brought in for heat exhaustion, right?"

At Drew's nod, Cale spun on his heel and headed toward the examination area.

"Where do you think you're going?" Drew asked, following his brother.

"I wanna see her."

"Why?"

Cale stopped and let out a stream of breath. "Curiosity. There's a damn good reason if you're hanging around a hospital when you don't have to be here." He repeated the words slowly, as if Drew was being deliberately obtuse. "I'm betting she's one hot reason, too."

Drew could continue to argue with Cale, thereby raising his brother's suspicions and determination, or he could drop the subject as if it held little importance. Either way, he knew from a lifetime of experience, Cale wouldn't back off until he'd thoroughly satisfied his curiosity.

Drew followed Cale through the electronic glass doors into the heart of the ER. Nurses, orderlies and physicians moved at a brisk pace between curtained partitions, through trauma room doors or hovered around a large horseshoe-shaped desk area, filling in charts, speaking on telephones or viewing lab reports in an efficient display of organized chaos. Positioned at the counter in a pair of mauve scrubs stood Tilly Jensen.

"Hey, Tils," Cale called to their childhood friend and neighbor. "Where's the woman Drew brought in? The heat exhaustion."

"Curtain three," she told Cale.

Tilly glanced up from the chart she'd been reading, her gaze intent on Drew. He and Tilly had been best buddies from the time he and his brothers first went to live with their aunt Debbie. Tilly's mother had died in childbirth, and the Perry boys had not only lost their mother, but their father, who had passed away less than two years later. The Perrys and Tilly had been kindred spirits, with Debbie Perry filling a void in all their lives.

"She's going to be fine." Tilly pushed a stray lock of her soft brown, chin-length hair behind her ear. "We don't think it was the heat, but we're waiting on labs just to be sure before we release her. It shouldn't be much longer, then you can take her home."

"Thanks," Drew said, oddly relieved, yet frustrated with himself for even harboring the emotion. Heat exhaustion or heatstroke could easily be fatal if not immediately treated. He ignored the knowing lift of his brother's eyebrows and attempted to convince himself the relief stemmed from the fact he'd been handy when Emily had needed someone with a modicum of medical training.

The argument was a hard sell, even to himself.

"What about her grandmother?" Drew asked. "Velma Norris?"

Tilly capped her pen and stuffed it into the front pocket of her scrubs. "She's staying the night. Her burn isn't too bad, but her doctor decided to keep her for observation as a precaution because of her age."

A doctor motioned for Tilly. "Curtain three," she said to Drew, pointing down a short corridor, before heading into another room.

Cale was unusually quiet as they neared Emily. Drew pushed through the opening in the curtain and his heart thumped heavily against his ribs.

Emily lay resting on a gurney. With her eyes closed and the cloud of wavy shoulder-length blond hair surrounding her face, she looked like something out of a fairy tale, waiting for the right guy to come along and kiss her awake so they could live happily ever after.

He didn't believe in fairy tales.

She must have sensed their presence. Her lashes fluttered, and then Drew found himself drawn into a pair of big soul-searching eyes the color of sweet, dark chocolate. Cale's assessment of *hot* didn't exactly sum up Drew's impression. *Breathtaking* did, however.

She looked from Drew to Cale, then back at Drew. The barest hint of a smile curved her lips. "Please, tell me I'm not seeing double."

"Nah." Cale stepped up to the gurney. "There's two of us. I'm Drew's older, much better-looking brother."

Drew ignored that comment and adjusted the head of the gurney for Emily as she attempted to sit upright. "Emily Dugan, my brother, Cale. The maladjusted middle child."

"Middle? You mean there's more of you?" Her gaze scanned them both again. "And you're both firemen?"

"Paramedic," Cale said. "Drew here likes to catch firebugs, and Ben, our oldest brother, he's the firefighter."

Emily frowned and looked at Drew. "You're an arson inspector?"

Cale slapped a hand down on Drew's shoulder. "Yup, he knows what a fire thinks."

"Don't you have somewhere to go?" Drew asked his brother.

"Not at the moment." Cale never could take a hint.

Drew decided to continue ignoring him. "Have they told you about your grandmother?" he asked Emily.

She nodded. "I'm going up to see her as soon as they release me. Do you know how it happened?"

He had a pretty good idea. Someone was setting fires. Until today, no one had been injured. Velma Norris's burns might not be life-threatening, but next time she might not be as fortunate.

"A fire was smoldering in the trash bin outside the school," Drew told Emily. "When your grandmother opened the bin, oxygen fed the flames. Her right hand and part of her forearm were injured."

Emily opened her mouth to say something just as a young doctor pushed through the curtain. He glanced at Emily, then at Drew and Cale. "Which one of you is responsible for the patient?"

"I am," Drew said, before he could stop himself. He wasn't *really* responsible for her, but he sure felt as if he'd been assigned the task of taking care of her. Exactly why, however, remained a mystery, especially since rescuing damsels in distress was Cale's gig, not his.

The doctor looked down at the chart, then back at Emily. "We have good news. Your labs came back in good order, and there were no signs of heatstroke. But I do suggest you take it easy and be sure to drink plenty of liquids as a precaution."

"May I leave now?" Emily asked, a hopeful note in her husky voice. The kind of voice that held the power to drift over a man's heart.

The doctor nodded, then tucked the chart under his arm. He gave Drew a stern look. "Don't leave her alone tonight. Just to be on the safe side...considering."

Drew frowned. "Considering?"

"Yes, considering her condition." The doctor smiled suddenly and extended his right hand to Drew. "You're going to be a father, Mr. Dugan. Congratulations!"

2

PREGNANT?

How on earth had that happened?

Emily wasn't stupid or naive. She knew all about the *how,* but the *whys* and *why nows* had her more than a little dumbfounded.

Alone on her grandmother's side of the semiprivate room, amid the get-well bouquets already arriving from friends and relatives, Emily lounged in the hard taupe vinyl chair and absently nibbled on her thumbnail while staring at the television screen where Pat Sajak interviewed the contestants on *Wheel of Fortune.* She hadn't spent five minutes alone with Grandy when an orderly had come and taken her away for therapy on her hand and arm, which was probably a good thing. At least Emily had a few minutes to herself to try to absorb the news the doctor had given her.

Drew had left, too. Well, run away was more like it after the doctor had mistakenly assumed she and Drew were together, not that she could blame the gorgeous arson inspector. She'd been as shocked by the news as Drew had been horrified by the doctor's assumption. Drew's brother had been highly amused, something which had brought a nurse in to ask Cale to leave because his chuckles were disturbing the other patients.

Drew had really surprised her when, despite everything, he'd told her he'd come back for her in a couple of hours so she'd have some time to visit her grandmother, no matter how much she'd insisted otherwise. Didn't she have enough problems without the unwanted attention of a handsome stranger, who was apparently very into playing Prince Valiant? Obviously someone thought her plate wasn't quite full enough.

Not that she was all that worried about it since she'd sworn off men, effective immediately.

She let out a sigh, her third in as many minutes. *Pregnant?* How on earth had *that* happened?

Better yet, how had her life managed to spin so completely out of control in virtually the blink of her eyes. She'd been a successful advertising executive, leading a creative team through a multibillion dollar ad campaign for a major department-store chain. She'd believed she was in a secure, stable and very comfortable long-term relationship, living together with her own supposed Mr. Right in an absolutely perfect two-bedroom, rent-controlled apartment on the west side. The next thing she knew, she was not only unemployed and single, but homeless and now pregnant, as well. All in the space of twenty-four hours.

Forget lemons. Life had handed her a whole basketful of limes, which everyone knew were much more bitter-tasting. In her state of impending motherhood, she didn't even have the luxury of being able to reach for the closest bottle of tequila and shaker of salt to make the best of a bad situation.

She nipped the skin surrounding her thumbnail and

winced. On the other side of the pink-and-gray striped curtain, Grandy's roomy snored softly while a very enthusiastic young woman bought vowels on the television. If Emily was feeling sorry for herself, which she wasn't, she figured even Shakespeare would be hard-pressed to write anything more tragic than the mess her life had become. Somehow, everything had managed to tilt so far off balance, she wondered if she dared tempt fate by holding even an ounce of hope that she might regain a modicum of control. She'd leapt from being a smart, savvy businesswoman with not only solid goals for her professional future, but with a finely detailed map of what she planned to accomplish in her personal life, onto an emotional roller coaster with more twists and turns than she could keep up with, even on a good day.

How in the world had *that* happened?

Before she did more damage to her thumb, she wrapped her arms around her middle and leaned forward in the chair. She was pregnant, something she figured would take her a little time to get used to.

But she'd been on birth control, for crying out loud. Why now, especially since her so-called boyfriend had dumped her for another woman just two hours before her flight to Los Angeles. For a junior partner in his law firm, he'd said. A woman more in tune with his professional needs.

Professional needs? The last time she'd looked, relationships were based on matters of the heart.

Charlie, now unaffectionately known as Cheatin' Charlie, hadn't even had the decency to end their relationship in private, but in the passenger check-in area of JFK Airport, of all places. Correction, he'd ended their relationship *and* informed her he would have her stuff moved into storage while she was in L.A. Considering she'd just been handed a pink slip the day before, along with twenty percent of the work force at Anderson and McIntyre Advertising because of corporate downsizing, she hadn't put up much of a fight. Yep, she'd gone from smart and savvy all right...straight to doormat.

Perhaps she'd just been too stunned to feel anything. With one striking blow after another, who could blame her? Even now, a dozen or so hours later, she still had a hard time mustering up anything close to an emotional outburst, angry, hurt or otherwise where Cheatin' Charlie Pruitt was concerned. Well, other than the fact that she'd decided to swear off men for a good long while. And for good reason, too.

Charlie wasn't the first bad choice she'd made in the relationship department. According to her small group of women friends, she was practically famous for her lousy choices. If she wanted to examine her twenty-seven-year history of relationships truthfully, which she most certainly did not, even she knew they were right. When it came to the opposite sex, she had a radar for men that were wrong for her, and the track record to substantiate the claim.

High school had been a series of dating disasters she'd tried hard to forget once she went away to college. She hadn't dated much her first couple of years, but her junior year she'd met and fallen head over heels for Rick Murdoch. He'd been premed, an all-American track star and vice president of the junior class. He'd also been stunningly gorgeous, just the kind of guy women spent hours drooling over in magazine ads. They'd had a lot in common, more than she'd ever imagined. Unfortunately, Rick turned out to be gay, something he decided right after she'd lost her virginity to him. How was she supposed to know the one thing they both *really* had in common was their attraction to men?

When she'd first moved to New York, after landing the account-rep job at Anderson and McIntyre, she'd actually met a wonderful guy who she was sure would make her forget about Rick. Jake was an actor, good-looking in a smooth pretty-boy sense. Attentive. A wicked sense of humor. And an absolutely incredible lover, which went a very long way in restoring the level of her battered sensuality-ego after the disaster of Rick.

She wasn't a perfectionist, not by a long shot. She understood people weren't perfect and came with quirks and baggage. Only there were some quirks she simply could not overlook. Jake turned out to have a taste for pornography she found a little too distasteful—like him being cast in the starring role of several X-rated films.

Then there'd been the guy who could never make a decision about anything unless he conferred with his mother first, followed by the borderline obsessive-compulsive who carried his own set of plastic ware to restaurants, something the maître d' at the Tavern on the Green had found so offensive, he'd asked them to leave. Alan Fontaine had had a few other idiosyncrasies regarding the physical aspect of relationships, as well, but she thought wearing surgical gloves while making love was taking things just a bit too far.

Finally a little over a year ago, she'd thought she'd finally found Mr. Right with Charles Pruitt, III. Tall, slender, with preppy Ken-doll good looks, he had a mesmerizing gaze filled with intelligence. He was a brilliant research attorney. Not a skin flick or latex glove in sight—that made him a plus. He had lacked any real sense of humor, but he had goals similar to her own, which made them work well together.

Turned out Cheatin' Charlie was really Mr. Not-A-Chance *and* the father of her baby.

Well, she thought resolutely, she wasn't the first woman to find herself pregnant and alone. As sure as the sun rose at dawn, she wouldn't be the last, either.

She shook her head, still trying to wrap her mind around the fact she was going to have a baby. It wasn't that she didn't want children, she was just...well, stunned. Starting a family had been part of her most recent five-year plan, but she'd hoped to have a husband, a home and a job first. She still had another couple of years before she figured she was ready to purchase a house, but she did have enough money saved that it wouldn't be a problem readjusting the real-estate portion of her plan. Provided she found another job first. The husband part, however, had just become moot. Good grief, she hadn't even realized she and Charlie were having problems.

She sat up straight and slid her hand over her tummy. A baby. Boy or girl? she wondered. Would her child look like her, or like Charlie? She had to admit, other than his rotten sense of timing and the fact that he'd apparently been cheating on her with Ms. Junior Partner, Charles Pruitt, III, wasn't all bad. A little too self-absorbed obviously, but not completely narcissistic. And they'd had a good time together. At least until she'd been assigned to lead the team of advertisers for the large ad campaign. She'd been keeping long hours for the last couple of months, and Charlie hadn't seemed to mind. Of course, she hadn't known he'd been otherwise occupied.

She hadn't even realized she was pregnant, and she couldn't help wondering what that said about her. When she'd become increasingly tired, she'd first suspected the long hours spent on the ad campaign had her run-down. She'd caught that wicked cold, followed by the flu, and had just never seemed to regain her usual verve. With her hectic and demanding work schedule, there hadn't been time to take off work to see a doctor for antibiotics, so Charlie had stocked her up on over-the-counter cold relievers. She'd managed to muddle through the cold, but the flu had left her feeling weak and tired much of the time.

"Oh my God," she whispered. That was it! That was the *how*—the antihistamines in all those over-the-counter flu and cold medications she'd been taking must have counteracted her birth-control pills.

A hysterical laugh bubbled up inside her, but she tamped it down lest she wake Grandy's roomy and the poor woman thought a lunatic was loose in the room. It might take two to tango, as the centuries-old saying went, but it looked as if Charlie was even more responsible for her newly acquired status as mother-to-be than she'd originally believed.

Cheatin' Charlie might have a skewed version of the meaning of monogamy, but he did know about responsibility. Of course, she couldn't tell him. He might be the father and he did deserve to know, but not now. Later, when he wouldn't dream of accusing her of stooping low enough to make a desperate attempt to hang on to a relationship that had gone south.

As for a place to live and finding gainful employment, she knew all she had to do was ask and she could temporarily room with either of her two dearest friends, Susan or Annie, until she found a job. She and Susan Carlson had been roommates in college, so it really wouldn't be much of an adjustment for either of them, especially since Susan traveled a great deal, thanks to her recent promotion in the public relations firm where she worked. Annie Pickett, on the other hand, a struggling actress who waited tables in between plays to pay the rent, would no doubt appreciate the financial assistance of a roommate.

Emily wasn't exactly destitute, but finding a job that paid as well as Anderson's would be difficult in the current job market. And an employer willing to hire a pregnant woman would be virtually nonexistent. Equal opportunities and discriminatory laws aside, when it came down to a final decision, why would someone hire her when she'd be taking a couple of months off for maternity leave within six or seven months of being hired?

She had a lot of thinking and planning to do. A natural list-maker, she reached into her purse for the small pad and pen she always carried with her and started making notes.

She was out of her home, out of a job and her man had dumped her.

Home, she wrote, followed by, Call Annie.

Job... Call headhunters.

Man. She made a noise and crossed that one off her list.

Baby. She tapped her pen, staring at the word, not having a clue where to begin.

A small smile curved her lips as she put pen to paper again.

Ashley, Adam.

Brandi, Brandon.

Chloe, Charles.

She drew a line through Charles. Carter.

Daisy, Drummond.

Eleanor, Ethan.

Fiona, Franklin.

Georgia...

DREW PARKED the state-issued, red Dodge Dynasty in the lot behind the firehouse, then took the rear entrance into Trinity Station. He headed up the back stairs to the second floor, avoided the bunkroom and walked straight to the deserted locker room. The guys who weren't out on calls would either be playing a few rounds of pinochle, watching the tube or catching some Z's before the next alarm sounded. Since he'd promised Emily he'd come back for her in a couple of hours, he didn't have time to guzzle coffee and shoot the breeze the way he usually did at the end of his shift. All he wanted was to change out of his uniform and take Emily back to her grandmother's house.

What came next, he couldn't say. He agreed with the doctor's opinion that Emily shouldn't be left alone tonight. She'd suffered a shock to her system, physically and definitely emotionally based on her stunned reaction to the announcement of her pregnancy. When he'd asked her if there was anyone he could call for her, she'd recovered enough from her surprise to give him a hard stare and emphatically state there was no one in her life to call.

He wasn't exactly certain what that meant, but one thing he did know, Emily Dugan was not his responsibility. Unfortunately that didn't prevent him from feeling otherwise. Not only had she fainted on him, but he'd gone and promised her grandmother he'd look after her. And a Perry's word was like oak—solid and unbreakable.

Before returning to the station, he'd gone back to the school to further inspect the damage. While he'd suspected an accelerant had been used, he'd been unprepared to find cooking oil coating the trash bin, which meant he had to consider Velma Norris as a suspect, at least temporarily. He didn't want to think the sweet old woman could be his firebug, but neither could he discount the evidence. The blaze hadn't been an accident. No one had simply disposed of old cooking oil. Someone had literally taken the time to coat the interior of the Dumpster. In his book, that spelled *arson*.

Firebugs weren't limited to a specific gender, age group or even social or economic status. In Drew's experience, there were usually four motivating factors for an arsonist. Vandalism was a typical one, and these fires were usually started by teens. Trash bins, like the one today, were often the most common starting point, and if it hadn't been for the two previous fires and the evidence he'd found at the cooking school, he might have discounted this latest incident to vandalism.

The motive to profit from an insurance claim, especially during hard economic times, as a way to escape a failing business or a big mortgage was likely, and something he had no choice but to consider. The place was definitely run-down, and from his two prior visits, he hadn't seen all that many students hanging around.

Revenge was often an arsonist's main objective, and usually an enraged, jilted lover or disgruntled employee was responsible for the burn. Actually, Drew considered revenge fire starters the most dangerous because of their emotional instability. They were also the easiest to catch, primarily because they were more concerned with the act of revenge than with hiding their crime. He'd considered this option briefly, but since there'd been no witnesses, he had his doubts this was the motive. Nor did he believe he was dealing with a garden-variety pyromaniac or even a firebug wanting to cover up another crime. Which brought him back to the answer he dreaded the most...fire for profit.

He tugged his shirt out of his trousers before he sat on the varnished wood bench to remove his work shoes. Reaching forward, he lifted the latch on his locker and opened the door. A basket tumbled out, followed by the plaintive cry of "Mama" from a child's doll. It sounded more like a braying lamb than a baby as it rolled over the concrete floor to his feet.

He leapt up and nearly toppled over the bench as a series of bubble-gum cigars in blue and pink fell from the top of the locker, raining over his head and shoulders. "What the..."

Snickers and the shuffling of feet echoed in the locker room. "All right, who's the comedian?" Drew called as he stooped to pick up the doll.

"Mama," the doll whined, followed by louder chuckles.

He turned to put the doll back in the basket, but set it on the bench instead, since the white wicker carrier that had held the little baby doll with blond ringlets was stuffed full of disposable diapers.

"Mama," the doll cried again.

Drew let out a sigh as his eye caught the shelf in his locker. Upon closer inspection, he realized the guys had replaced his shampoo with a no-more-tears formula of baby shampoo. Instead of his black comb was an infant's brush and comb in pink, with tiny blue flowers no less. His bar of soap had disappeared, too, but his co-workers had included a bottle of baby soap, along with economy-size bottles of pink baby lotion and talcum powder.

"You can come out now," he said. He suspected Cale was responsible for the joke since he'd been with him when Emily's doctor had mistakenly assumed Drew was "the responsible party." A big joke at that, since marriage and family were absolutely not part of his lifelong agenda. He might have one of the lower-risk jobs in the fire department, but he still faced a good amount of danger investigating fires each time he entered a burned-out structure. Since he had no intention of hanging up his gear, he'd decided a long time ago there was no way he'd put a child or a wife through one ounce of the pain he'd suffered at the loss of his parents.

"Drew, buddy," Tom "Scorch" McDonough said as he rounded the corner. A wide grin split the paramedic's freckled face. "You should have told us."

Cale slapped Drew on the back. "He's been keeping this one quiet."

Drew shrugged off his brother's hand. "Hey, I hardly know her."

"Wow." Fitz, another third-generation firefighter, laughed. "That's fast work. Even for you."

Cale crossed his arms and leaned against the row of lockers, careful to avoid the bubble-gum cigars littering the floor. "Yeah, but you're interested. I saw the look, Drew."

He frowned. "What look?" Since when had he become so transparent that Cale could tell what he was thinking?

"The one you get when your interest is piqued by someone of the opposite sex," Brady, Cale's paramedic partner, added.

Scorch nodded knowingly. "That starving-dog look."

"More like a lovesick-puppy look," Ben Perry said.

Drew shot them all a scathing glance, then tugged his T-shirt over his head and tossed it in the bottom of the locker. "I'm doing an old woman a favor. End of story."

A slight smile curved Ben's mouth, something that didn't happen often enough. "Sounds like the beginning of one to me."

Drew shucked out of his trouser and briefs, then picked up a clean towel to wrap around his waist. "Shows how much you *don't* know. Now if you comedians will excuse me, I need to shower and get back to the hospital." He turned his back on the practical jokers, shrugged and grabbed the bottle of baby shampoo from the shelf. Shampoo was shampoo, after all.

"See what I mean?" Cale said.

"He can't stand to be away from her," Brady added.

Scorch laughed. "Looks like his Casanova days are numbered."

Drew stopped in front of the last locker at the end of the row and turned to face them. He could give and take with the best of them, and had even been the engineer behind more than a practical joke or two. But they'd just gone too far in his mind. No way in hell were his bachelor days in danger of disappearing. He enjoyed women, a lot, and preferred the freedom of sampling all they had to offer too much to be tied down to only one woman.

"You guys should talk," he told them. "Cale's engaged, Brady's wife is pregnant and not talking to him again, and Scorch is tied up in knots over Tilly. Now whose days are numbered?" He couldn't blame a woman for putting Ben through the wringer. As far as Drew knew, the last time his older brother had gone on a date was at least three, maybe even four, months ago.

Cale grinned. "Not Scorch. Tilly's ticked off at him. Again."

"What'd you do this time?" Ben asked Scorch. "Forget the one-month anniversary of your first date or something?"

Scorch shoved a hand through his permanent case of bed-head carrot-red hair. "Worse," he admitted. "Her birthday."

"Aw jeez. You're screwed," Fitz offered sympathetically. "I missed Krista's birthday once and let me tell you, it's gonna take some major sucking up. Think jewelry, pal."

Scorch let out a sigh and rubbed the back of his head. "She hated the flowers I brought her today. She threw them at me. Plastic vase and all."

Drew grinned triumphantly. "See what I mean? Until you idiots can get your love lives straightened out, don't even think about lecturing me on mine."

Not that he had a love life that included Emily Dugan. Then again, she *had* made it crystal clear she was single. When it came to women, Drew was always open to exploring the possibilities...of anything short-term, of course.

3

NIGHT MIGHT HAVE FALLEN over Southern California, but the disappearance of the blazing sun didn't mean the sizzling temperatures had bothered to follow suit by more than a degree or two. By the time Emily had walked from Drew's black SUV to the brick steps of her grandmother's house, her calf-length cotton floral dress was already starting to cling uncomfortably to her back.

"You really don't have to do this," she told Drew, for what had to be the fifth time since he'd returned to the hospital for her. Once she'd bidden her grandmother good-night, Drew had given her a choice: his place or hers. The devil had even tried to blackmail her, threatening to tattle to Grandy about the baby if she refused. His underhanded, and quite effective, tactic had worked like a charm, too. How on earth he'd known she hadn't uttered a single word about the day's events to Grandy was beyond her, but not wanting to upset her grandmother had Emily complying without much of a fight. Since she'd already informed the hospital staff they could reach her here if Grandy's condition should change during the night, she'd reluctantly agreed to let him stay. Not that she expected anything to go wrong. Grandy might be in her twilight years, but the old gal was still as strong, and twice as stubborn, as an ox.

Drew's hand settled on her sweaty back as she carefully made her way in the dark to the porch. The tingles chasing up and down her spine like the crazed lights of a pinball machine had nothing whatsoever to do with sexual attraction. No, those little pinpricks of excitement were merely caused by the surprise of an unexpected touch.

Could have happened to anyone. Uh-huh. That was her story. And dammit, she was sticking to it.

"Do you have the key?" Drew asked, tugging open the wood-framed screened door.

Thank heavens she'd only have to suffer his presence until morning, she thought. If the sound of that low, sexy rumble in his voice just asking for a stupid key had the power to put her feminine senses on alert, she hated to think what her reaction would be when he asked her where he'd be sleeping for the night.

She withdrew Grandy's key ring from her purse and handed it to Drew. Within seconds, he held the door for her and she walked past him into the cozy and, she noted thankfully, air-conditioned living room. Warm light from the automatic-timed lamp bathed the area with the same welcoming sense of coming home she always experienced whenever she returned for a visit, which hadn't been nearly often enough in the last couple of years. She'd been busy building her career.

And for what? she wondered with an unexpected stab of bitterness. Just to receive a pink slip and a somewhat decent severance package that would tide her over for a couple of months before she'd be forced to dig into her savings? A fat lot of good all those long hours had done her.

While Drew brought in her bags, which they'd left stowed on the porch during her unexpected visit to the emergency room, Emily tried to forget her employment status for the time being. Instead, she breathed in the familiar scents of lemon wax, the faint aroma of cinnamon from the big jar candle resting on the mantel of the small brick fireplace, and something that smelled suspiciously like fresh-baked cookies. Oatmeal-raisin cookies.

The ancient tole-painted wooden box nestled near the fireplace still housed various cars and trucks handcrafted by her grandfather for her male cousins and half brother, along with a pair of well-loved baby dolls once shared by her, her half sister and a handful of female Norris cousins. The requisite coloring books and a fat round Christmas tin filled to the brim with crayons of every shade imaginable, now shared by the next generation, rested on top of the pile of toys. A generation, she suddenly realized, that would include her own child in a matter of months.

She needed time to come to terms with what had happened, which was why she hadn't yet shared the news with her grandmother. Besides, if the state of disrepair around the property was any indication, Grandy had plenty enough to concern herself with and didn't need to add worry over her unwed, pregnant granddaughter. Once Grandy was released from the hospital, and Emily assured herself that the time was right—when she had a firm plan in mind on exactly what she was going to do next—she'd tell her grandmother about the baby, about her loss of employment and all about Cheatin' Charlie. So far, only she and Drew, along with Drew's brother Cale, knew of her status as mother-to-be. In Emily's opinion, that was already two too many people.

The screen door snapped shut, drawing her attention. "Where do you want these?" Drew asked her.

Her vocal chords refused to function at the sight of all that corded male arm muscle straining with the weight of her suitcases gripped in his large hands. She stared, fascinated.

"Emily? You're not going to faint on me again are you?"

She shook her head, and pointed toward the hallway off the living room.

"Which room?" he called from the corridor.

"Second on the left," she managed to answer. Apparently her capacity for speech worked just fine when she wasn't staring at him like a loon.

Her tummy grumbled, reminding her she hadn't had a thing to eat since her flight.

She headed into the kitchen in search of sustenance. In the fridge, as she suspected, Grandy had stocked up on Emily's favorites. She considered a bowl of cottage cheese with fresh sliced strawberries and some dry toast, but didn't think her self-appointed guardian would consider her choices much by way of a real meal. She dug a little deeper, found some American cheese slices and set them on the counter.

"Have you eaten?" she asked Drew when he saun-tered into the kitchen. She didn't possess one iota of her grandmother's culinary gene, but she'd been known to manage just fine with a grilled cheese sand-wich and a can of soup. Occasionally. If she was really, really careful.

"Actually, no." He pulled a cell phone from the pocket of his trousers. "I thought we could order in. Maybe some Thai or Italian."

She appreciated the thought, but wrinkled her nose just the same. Besides, she didn't trust her stomach with food quite that solid or spicy. "Something a little less exotic, please. How does grilled cheese and a can of soup sound?"

The sexy tilt of his mouth, combined with the charm-ing glint in his eyes, had her pulse revving all over again. How was it possible for one man to possess so much blatant sexual magnetism? It was a test, she de-cided. She'd sworn off men and she was being tested by some unseen entity with a wicked sense of humor. Well, she'd never flunked a test in her life, and she wasn't about to start now. Her life had become a disas-ter within a twenty-four-hour period. She shouldn't even be lusting after some guy, no matter how hot and bothered just looking at him made her.

"Boring," he said. That way-too-charming smile never wavered.

He started pressing buttons on his phone then reached for the pad of paper and pen her grandmother kept handy on the counter.

Emily stepped as close as humanly possible to the

open refrigerator, hoping the cool blast of air would quell those hot, hot images spurring to life. A wasteful wish if one ever existed.

"Would a BLT be exciting enough for you?" Maybe she could even manage to convince him to fry up the bacon since she usually charred the stuff beyond recognition. The beauty of living in New York was that just about anything could be delivered practically every hour of the day, even a BLT. A service she took advantage of plenty on a regular basis.

While Drew continued to jot down phone numbers, she wondered if Cheatin' Charlie's new lady lawyer cooked for him.

Drew flipped his cell phone shut and slipped it back inside his pocket, then shrugged those incredible linebacker-wide shoulders. "Why not? Want some help?"

This man had to have angel wings hidden somewhere on his body. Too bad she wasn't interested— much. Obviously her pregnancy-induced hormones were running rampant because she had a feeling exploring that heavenly body to find them could be a whole lot of fun. "You do the bacon, I'll do the rest."

While Drew started the bacon, she avoided anything to do with actual meal preparation and set the table. Her tummy grumbled again thanks to the mouthwatering scents floating on the air. Thankfully Drew's good manners kept him from commenting. Her own good manners fled the scene when she caught sight of the notepad on the counter.

She counted. Thirteen telephone numbers? And the names of *thirteen* different women.

Thirteen?

She glanced over her shoulder at Drew. *Thirteen?*

"Excuse me?"

"Uh..." She hadn't realized she'd even spoken out loud. "You always this popular, or are you running a sale?"

He turned his head slightly to the side, a bewildered expression on his handsome face. "What are you talking about?"

She rolled her eyes. What had her first impression of him been? Oh yeah. A charmer. The kind of man incredibly dangerous to women who made a habit of picking the wrong guy. The kind she'd never be so foolish to ever fall for again. Especially when he was the kind who collected messages from thirteen different women.

She picked up the pad of paper and started reading. "Leanne, Karenna, Dora, Elise, Sophia and, oh— please—Tiffany?" She laughed and continued reading. "Wendy, Frenchie? Gee, I wonder what she's known for. Debbie, Amanda, Tilly, Nina, and..."

She peered closer, but the last name was nearly illegible. "H.B? What is that? Code for hot babe?"

A true scoundrel's grin curved his mouth, and heaven help her, she almost found him irresistible.

"No," he said, his voice coated with humor. "It's shorthand for Hannah's Bakery."

She dropped the tablet back on the counter, pretending disgust. "I don't think I want to know what baked goods and a baker's dozen of women have in common."

"Since you asked—"

"I didn't."

The teasing glint in his eyes said otherwise. "Debbie is my aunt," he explained. "Amanda is my brother's fiancée and Tilly is my best friend."

She pulled plates and soup mugs from the cabinet. "Strange name for a guy."

"Probably because she's a woman."

Now why wasn't she surprised to learn a sweet-talking, drop-dead gorgeous specimen of male perfection had a woman for a best friend?

"Debbie called to see if I could pick up the cake for Amanda's bridal shower at the bakery by noon on Sunday," he said.

"You really don't have to explain."

"Tilly," he said, ignoring her, "wanted to let me know she'd taken care of Cale and Amanda's wedding present, and my future sister-in-law wanted to know if I'd been able to find the gift *she* wants to give my oldest brother to celebrate his promotion to lieutenant."

Emily handed him the dishes then crossed her arms and looked at him skeptically. "Let me guess. You want me to believe you're really related to the other women on that list, right?"

He shrugged and his grin turned sheepish.

What did she care anyway? She'd sworn off men.

Well, she had!

Fifteen minutes later they were seated at the round oak table in the corner of the kitchen. Drew had unearthed sliced turkey in the fridge, and rather than BLTs, they shared the best turkey Newburg on toasted

English muffins she'd ever tasted, expertly prepared by Drew. Which sure beat anything she could've created in the kitchen. Almost anything was preferable to her cooking, a term she used loosely.

Emily looked across the table at Drew. The man really was way too sexy for her own good, but she couldn't think about that now. Or ever, and she firmly reminded her wayward hormones of that telling list of women. There were questions that had been simmering in the back of her mind all afternoon that required answers. With everything that had gone on, there hadn't really been an opportunity to talk to him privately and when she'd had the chance, she'd allowed herself to be sidetracked by that harem of his.

"Why would a garbage-can fire necessitate an arson inspection?" she asked him suddenly.

He took a bite of his meal and chewed instead of giving her an answer, making her wonder if he'd even heard her.

"I noticed some charred crates, too," she continued. "And soot stains near the exit. The fire today wasn't the first, was it?"

Drew let out a sigh and set his fork on the delicate china plate. He'd expected her questions sooner or later. He'd just wished it'd been later, when he had some solid answers. "You're not a reporter, are you?"

"No. I'm..." She paused and let out a short huff of breath. "I *was* an advertising executive."

"Was?" he prompted, attempting to steer the conversation into a more personal direction. Emily intrigued him, but then most women did on one level or another, so he wasn't overly concerned.

"Corporate downsizing." She dismissed the subject with a wave of her hand. "The fires?"

So much for a redirection of topic, he thought, although he planned a revisit shortly. He wanted to know more about this absent father of her baby, which should be reason enough to ignore the faint stirring of need in his gut whenever he looked into Emily's big brown eyes. Only he couldn't seem to help himself.

"Today was the third incident," he told her.

Her eyes widened in disbelief. "The third?" She shook her head as if trying to absorb the information. "Grandy never said a word to me about the fires."

Maybe because she was guilty as hell. "Maybe she didn't want to worry her family," he said instead.

Emily set her plate aside and rested her arms over the oak table. Her frown made a reappearance. He'd known plenty of women in his lifetime, and not a single one of them looked half as tempting as Emily Dugan when they frowned.

"What else has happened?" she demanded. "How long has this been going on?"

"Maybe you should talk to your grandmother about it." He wasn't concerned with putting his investigation at risk by sharing information with her, but he did feel she should be talking to Velma rather than to him. Under normal circumstances, they wouldn't even be having this conversation.

"And let Grandy excuse the incidents as insignificant little nuisances? Not a chance." Her big soulful

eyes filled with determination that matched the firm-
ness of her tone. "Besides, any investigation performed
by the fire department is a matter of public record.
Which translates to you not being in danger of breach-
ing confidentiality laws by telling me what's been going on around here. If someone is trying to hurt my
grandmother, then I have a right to know."

She had him there. "What makes you think someone
else is responsible?"

Her mouth formed a perfectly shaped "O" before
her gaze narrowed. "You can't possibly believe an
eighty-year-old woman is responsible for setting those
fires? That's absolutely insane."

He leaned back in the chair, enjoying the heat in her
voice a whole lot more than was prudent. She was, after all, carrying another man's child, which classified
Emily as strictly taboo, no matter how much she intrigued him. A guy did need to have his standards, and
lusting after another man's woman went against his
own set of values. Unless the guy had indeed pulled a
disappearing act.

"Is it?" he asked. "Have you taken a good look
around? This place is falling apart."

"That does not mean my grandmother is an arsonist!"

He shrugged and bit back a smile. Too bad such an
exciting woman was off-limits. *Maybe* off-limits.

"Yes, it could, especially if the property is heavily
mortgaged and she wants out. Believe me, Emily. People start fires for a variety of reasons, and a huge pay-

off by their insurance company to get out from under a large debt is right there at the top of the list."

"Well, not in this case," she retorted. "Grandy and Pop paid off the property years ago."

"Do you know for certain she's never mortgaged it?"

"No," she admitted. "I don't. Not for certain, but it's highly unlikely. Grandy would never risk the school or her home."

Deep down, he agreed with her. Velma Norris hardly came across as the criminal type: she appeared to be quite sharp and seemed to be a savvy business-woman despite her advanced age. Yet, the subject still required a thorough investigation, if for no other reason than to clear her of any wrongdoing.

"Drew, would you please tell me what's going on?"

He sat forward and braced his arms on the table. "As I said, today was the third incident. The first fire happened about two weeks ago and looked to be nothing more than a grease fire that had flared out of control in one of the classrooms. No one was hurt, but according to your grandmother, the classroom was deserted when the fire started. It looked like someone had acci-dentally spilled grease beneath the top of the range and it was ignited by a faulty pilot light."

"That doesn't make much sense," Emily said as she began to stack their dirty dishes. "Grandy has those ranges checked by the gas company once a month to prevent something like that from happening."

He filed that information away for later, and made a

note to contact the gas company to check out the service records.

"Last week the department received a call from a neighbor who spotted smoke billowing from the back of the school. Those charred crates you noticed behind the building? They were filled with old newspapers. A lit cigarette was the cause."

Emily stood and carried the dishes to the sink. "Grandy doesn't smoke," she said, turning on the tap. "Couldn't it have just been an accident? A careless student maybe?"

Drew pushed away from the table and joined Emily at the sink. At least standing next to her he wasn't quite as prone to sit and ogle the seductive curve of her derriere. "I might believe that if the cigarette had been tossed on the top. But this was tucked inside in a way that leads me to believe it was intentional."

He took the dish towel Emily handed him before she sank her hands into the soapy water. "The fire today was the most obvious. Someone took the time to coat the trash bin with cooking oil then set a rag on fire and toss it inside. Your grandmother didn't realize there was something smoldering inside the bin and when she opened it, oxygen fed the flames. She could've been seriously injured."

Emily glanced up and handed him a plate to dry. "All of which should eliminate her as a suspect, don't you think?"

He shrugged. "Unless she's the one responsible."

"You can't be serious."

"Off the record, I have my doubts."

"Doubts?" Her expression said loud and clear what she thought of his doubts. "Whatever happened to common sense?"

He set the dried plate on the counter, then lifted another from the drain board. "Every possibility has to be considered, Emily. She refuses to close the school despite my recommendation to do so. Someone is setting these fires, and until the firebug is apprehended, no one is above suspicion. Not even your grandmother."

She let out another little breath and shifted her attention back to washing dishes. "I just can't imagine who would do such a thing. Or why, for that matter. Grandy has to be one of the most generous, kindest people on the planet. Why would anyone want to hurt her?"

Any number of reasons, he thought to himself. Firebugs didn't do things that made sense in the logical scheme of things, except in their own twisted minds where their actions were justified. So far only Velma had been present on the property when the fires started.

For obvious reasons, he didn't like the idea of Emily and her grandmother staying alone with an arsonist on the loose, if Velma wasn't the one responsible. He couldn't very well move in with them until the culprit was apprehended. Besides, he didn't get involved. Period. Saving damsels in distress had been Cale's gig until Amanda had come into his life. Just because he had retired his white charger, didn't mean it was Drew's job to pick up where Cale had left off. Not a chance. Drew was only staying the night because he'd been rendered temporarily insane.

Emily drained the sink and started putting the dishes he'd dried into the cabinets.

He crossed his ankles and leaned against the counter, enjoying the delectable view of her backside. "Mind if I ask how long you're planning to visit?" he asked her.

She drew in a deep breath, effectively drawing his gaze to the rise and fall of her breasts. Her very full breasts.

"Initially, only one month." After closing the cabinet, she turned to look at him. "Suddenly I find myself in not much of a hurry to return to New York."

He nodded slowly, struggling to ignore the itch in his palms to feel the weight of her breasts against his hand. "The corporate downsizing?"

She braced her hands behind her and leaned against the gleaming countertop. "For starters. I think there's a black cloud following me around."

He chuckled when she wrinkled her nose in that cute way of hers. "It can't be all that bad."

A wry, self-deprecating grin curved her lips. "It's a good thing I have a sense of humor because I definitely hit the double trifecta today. Not only am I out of a job, I got dumped—at the airport of all places—and since I gave up my rent-controlled apartment six months ago to move in with my now ex, I'm out of my home."

She folded the dish towel and draped it over the drain board. "If that's not enough to heap on one person within twenty-four hours," she continued, "I also discover I'm going to have a baby, my grandmother's in the hospital and now you're telling me that someone is trying to burn down her life's work." She shook her head and managed a short burst of laughter that held little humor. "I'm almost afraid to ask, what's next?"

He wondered if she had any idea how her eyes brightened when she laughed. Or how his gut just tightened with need at her announcement that there was no longer a man in her life. Which could very well be a temporary situation for all he knew. Besides, once she told the guy about the baby, in Drew's opinion, there was a pretty strong chance the guy would be back in her life again, provided he had any sense of responsibility.

"Wanna talk about it?" He resisted the ridiculous need to look out the kitchen window to see if a white steed was grazing nearby.

"And spread around my doom and gloom? Thanks, but no thanks." She pushed off the counter. "I've had about as much as I can stand for one day."

He flipped off the light switch and followed her out of the kitchen into the living room. "It's not healthy to keep things inside."

He'd bet his trust fund he'd just heard the clank of armor.

She sat in a wooden rocking chair near the fireplace and looked up at him. Curiosity filled her eyes. "Why are you being so nice to me? You don't even know me. Obviously you're not short on dates, so it's not as if you're hard up for female companionship."

He winced at the reminder of his overloaded voice-

mail box. No answer—at least none he cared to admit—sprang to mind.

He shrugged, then took a seat on the sofa. "I made a
promise," he answered evasively. Not exactly the
truth, but he sure didn't want to tell her that, in his
opinion, she far outranked those other women on the
intelligence scale. And then, of course, he did enjoy her
sense of humor. Better yet, she didn't appear to want
anything from him, either. From what he knew of her
thus far, she didn't strike him as the type of woman to
play games and she most certainly said whatever was
on her mind. Traits, he realized, that were downright
refreshing.

"You made a promise to an emergency-room doctor
you don't even know, and to a woman you think could
be an arson suspect. Really, Drew. You don't have to
do this. In fact, I'd feel more comfortable if you went
home."

"I don't mind."

"Well, I do. I'm not willing to be added to your col-
lection."

"Too bad," he said, and damned if he didn't mean it
in spite of himself. Of course, nothing long-term. "I'm
not leaving."

"Don't you have phone calls to return?"

The frown tugging her eyebrows together made her
look cute and spunky. He'd dated cute plenty. He'd
even had spunky, but never had he seen such a tempting, wicked combination.

He grinned in response.

She pushed out of the chair. "Suit yourself. There's a

guest room across from mine. Make yourself at home. I'm going to take a hot shower and go to bed."

"Good night, Emily," he called softly after her.

She muttered something that could've been a goodnight, but he couldn't say for certain.

Drew sat in the quiet of the living room until he heard the water running from the shower. He could call any number of women to satisfy his needs. But none of them interested him tonight. Not when he couldn't seem to get his mind off the image of Emily's slender body standing beneath the stinging spray, or the way her hot, moist skin would feel against his. He reached for the remote control and turned on the television. As far as Friday nights went, he couldn't recall when he'd last spent a night watching the tube— alone—especially when there was a beautiful, exciting woman within reach.

Even if the woman occupying his thoughts was strictly off-limits.

Maybe.

4

"HMM, DREW," Emily whispered, then laced her fingers together behind his neck to pull his mouth down to hers for a hot, openmouthed, all-consuming kiss.

Somewhere in her subconscious she understood she was lost inside a delicious dream, but the warmth of his lips against hers couldn't be any more real than if she'd actually kissed him.

Her tongue sought and mated with his, while her body arched against the rough maleness of his bare skin. She breathed in his arousing scent, then moaned from the intoxicating wickedness of forbidden pleasure. He murmured something against her mouth. She shoved her hands into his hair and applied pressure to quiet him. If he stopped kissing her, she'd...

"Wake up, Emily."

Her eyes flew open, and she found herself nose to nose with Drew.

Uh-oh. What *had* she done?

Reality crashed into her. If there was a rock nearby, she'd certainly crawl beneath it and never come out again. Once she pulled her arms from around his neck, of course.

The deliciously wicked dream hadn't been a figment

of her overly erotic subconscious at all, but instead deliciously wicked…and as real as it got!

Her lips were still warm and moist. Oh. Oh! What had she done? She'd kissed him, that's what. And since her luscious dream had had more than an hint of reality coursing through it, he'd kissed her back, too.

Slowly, she lowered her arms and muttered an apology. If he didn't have her trapped between his gloriously wide *naked* chest and the mattress, she would've scooted as far away from him as humanly possible.

She didn't think she'd ever been more horrified in her life than to awaken to discover that her hot and sexy dream, starring a hot and sexy arson inspector, hadn't been a dream at all. Her only hope, and an excruciatingly slim one at that, was that he had no idea she'd actually been dreaming about *him*.

She flopped back against the mound of pillows and slapped her hand over her eyes. "God, I am so sorry," she said more clearly this time. "I don't know what…" She peeped at him through her fingers and frowned. "Wait a minute." It was one thing for her subconscious to go all gaga over a man she hardly knew, but quite another when he showed up in her bed—half-naked and uninvited. "What are you doing in here anyway?"

"We have to go."

"Go?" She'd been on her way to heaven when he'd woken her.

He nodded and shoved a lock of mussed hair from his eyes. Lord, he looked rumpled and sexy and way too yummy for a woman in her position—flat on her back with her body primed from an undeniably hot dream.

"The hospital called," he said solemnly. "It's your grandmother."

The last vestiges of embarrassment, along with the twinge of self-righteous indignation she'd been working up, evaporated. "What's happened?"

"Apparently she didn't bother to call for a nurse and took a fall. It looks like she's broken her ankle."

THROUGH THE narrow, oblong window above her grandmother's hospital bed in the intensive care unit, Emily had watched the colors of the sky change from the dark of night to the gray of early dawn, followed by the brilliance of the morning sun promising yet another scorching summer day. By two in the afternoon, Mother Nature had kept her word, delivering temperatures in the triple digits.

When she and Drew had arrived at the hospital early that morning, the doctors had assured her they expected her grandmother to have a full recovery. They had her scheduled for surgery at 8:00 a.m. that day to repair the severe damage to the ankle.

Due to Grandy's age, they'd taken her to the ICU following surgery. The orthopedist, a far cry older than the twelve-year-old ER doctor Emily had seen the previous day, had been patient in explaining the procedure and the recovery process. Once the cast and pins were removed from her ankle in about six weeks, Grandy would require physical therapy. All in all, she'd been fortunate in that she hadn't broken her hip.

Just the same, her recovery would be a slow one, again due to her advanced years.

Regardless of the assurances by the hospital staff, Emily still worried. Much of her childhood had been spent with her grandmother, and in her opinion, Grandy had been more of a mother to her than her own mother.

Glynis Norris was a true product of the free-spirited free-love generation of her time. It still amazed Emily that her mother had even bothered to marry Tommy Dugan, although the ink on Emily's birth certificate had barely dried before her parents had filed for divorce. She didn't know her father, but she still counted herself the lucky one, since Glynis hadn't bothered to marry the fathers of Emily's half brother and half sister.

Emily preferred solidity and security in her life, while her mother had been born with wanderlust in her veins. It hadn't been long after she'd returned home to her parents with a newborn daughter in tow that she'd taken off for a commune in Oregon. She'd carted Emily with her, but before reaching the ripe old age of five, Emily ended up living with Grandy and Pop, where she'd remained much of her life. At least until those rare occasions when her mother's latent maternal instincts made an uncharacteristic reappearance.

How Emily had hated those times. Unlike her mother, she enjoyed knowing where she'd be sleeping each night, preferably in her own bed, in her own room. By the time she'd reached puberty, the animosity between mother and daughter had grown to such an uncomfortable level, Glynis declared it better for "everyone's spirit" if Emily remained permanently with her grandparents. An arrangement which had suited Emily just fine.

Her half siblings, Duke and Justine, had inherited more of their mother's adventurous spirit and had remained with Glynis for much of their childhoods, but occasionally there would be times when they, too, would be sent to stay with Grandy and Pop. Every once in a while, Duke or Justine would be shuttled off to their respective fathers, but those visits rarely lasted longer than a week or two before her brother and sister would end up back at Grandy and Pop's again.

Emily *loved* those times. She adored her younger brother and sister, and regretted that she'd not seen them much since she'd moved to New York under the obviously misguided impression that she'd conquer the advertising world. Duke called Alabama home, but traveled on the auto-racing circuit. The guy was an absolute whiz with engines and was currently the pit-crew chief for one of the country's top stock-car racing teams. A longing for roots had eventually tamed Justine's adventuresome spirit. For the past two years she'd been happy working as a ranch hand in Wyoming. Last Emily had heard, her mother was an artist's assistant in New Mexico. But that was over three months ago. Knowing Glynis as she did, she figured her mother could be anywhere by now.

She'd already spoken to Justine, who'd promised to track down Duke and let him know about Grandy. Emily's two uncles, Tyler and John, lived out of state and had promised to come right away if necessary. Her cousins were scattered around the country, so for the moment, the responsibility of seeing to Grandy's needs fell to her.

And so she quietly sat while her grandmother slept off the effects of anesthesia. Drew seemed to be dozing in the reclining chair in the far corner of the room.

She simply didn't understand this man. Not only were they strangers, he was technically investigating her grandmother as a possible arsonist, yet he'd remained by Emily's side, stoically offering her his silent support when he could be otherwise occupied with at least ten other women...literally. Yet, not once had he expressed an ounce of impatience or so much as a hint that he wanted to be anywhere but with her while she kept vigil over her grandmother.

She made a little huffing sound. Charlie would've made sure his cell phone was turned on and told her she could call him if she wanted to should Grandy's condition worsen.

A very young and pretty nurse came quietly into the small room, moving silently around Grandy's bed, checking monitors, thermal graphs and the IV drip, taking care not to awaken the sleeping patient. The nurse smiled warmly in Drew's direction. No surprise there since women apparently fell at the man's feet. Emily included, if she counted her fainting episode yesterday.

The nurse nodded to her, signaling all was well, then slipped out of the room as quietly as she'd entered, shooting one last adoring glance in Drew's direction.

The unsuspecting male stirred, opened his eyes and looked directly at Emily. A sleepy smile tipped his mouth, making her grateful she wasn't the one hooked up to those monitors. The lines on the thermal graph would've zigzagged straight off the narrow little chart.

"You should go home," she said, keeping her voice low so as not to disturb her grandmother. Women were probably camped out on his doorstep.

"So should you," he answered.

"But you've done far too much already. Really, you can leave. I'll be fine." Maybe then her pulse would stop red-lining like the tachometer on one of Duke's race-car engines.

There wasn't a single logical explanation for all the silly heart pounding and pulse racing going on, either. For heaven's sake. Hadn't she just been dumped by one more in a long line of lousy choices? She had absolutely no business getting all mushy inside just because Drew looked like a nice guy.

A nice guy who'd kissed her back when she'd been acting out the physical aspects of an erotic dream. Something he'd been kind enough to not mention.

See? A nice guy. Right there in front of you. Not all of them are big, stupid jerks.

She wasn't buying it. Not from a guy that had far too many phone numbers, probably all on speed dial. If there was any truth to the rumor that nice guys did exist, then her heart wouldn't be carrying around battle scars which proved otherwise. Even so, she barely managed to contain the sigh just dying to escape.

Given enough time, she thought cynically, big, stupid-male jerkdom would eventually find its way through all that charm and those sexy good looks. Forget his crowded voice mail box. She had her own history with men which practically demanded it.

"I have a better idea," her grandmother said suddenly, taking Emily by surprise. A gentle smile and affection banked in her gaze took the bite out of her words. "Both of you go home so I can get some rest."

Emily scooted to the edge of the chair and took her grandmother's hand. "I'm sorry we woke you."

Grandy made a swishing motion with her free hand. "You didn't." She turned her attention to Drew. "Inspector Perry, what are you doing here?"

Drew pushed out of the chair and came up to the opposite side of the bed. "Making sure you don't start racing up and down the halls," he said, turning on the charm.

Her grandmother blushed like a high-school freshman who'd finally been noticed by the senior hotshot. Emily didn't quite know what to think about that. The last time she'd seen her grandmother blush had been when Emily had walked into the kitchen looking for a snack and had caught her grandparents sharing a passionate kiss. Grandy had been flustered and embarrassed, but not Pop. He'd grinned like a randy old fool. If it hadn't been for her grandparents' marriage, Emily might have given up completely on the idea of happily ever after. In the ten years since her grandfather's passing, Velma Norris hadn't so much as looked at another man, let alone blush because of some gentle teasing by a sweet-talking charmer.

"It's going to be a few days before I'm ready for that race," Grandy said, her voice surprisingly strong. She looked over at Emily. "I've gone and ruined your visit, haven't I?"

"No, you haven't," Emily assured her. "And there's no reason why we can't visit right here until you're released."

Emily thought she felt her grandmother attempt to give her hand a squeeze, but the movement was so slight, she couldn't be sure. Which only served to remind her that perhaps her grandmother wasn't quite as strong as Emily wanted to believe.

"I want you to go home and get some rest. You look horrid, dear. You can come back in the morning, and when you do, please bring my address book. I need to find a substitute to take over my classes."

"Grandy, don't think about that now," she chastised gently. "You're supposed to concentrate on getting well."

Drew pulled his beeper from his side.

"It's my responsibility," Grandy said in that determined way of hers that told Emily she'd be wasting her breath to argue. "Margo and Rita don't have the time to take on extra classes and there are about a dozen students who've already paid tuition for my Elegant Desserts and the Creams and Sauces classes, which begin on Monday."

"Grandy—"

Drew cleared his throat, stopping Emily before she wasted that breath. "If you'll excuse me, I need to make a call."

Emily waited until Drew disappeared. "Grandy, I don't think you should be worrying about this now. Besides, Margo and Rita are both more than qualified to cover your classes."

Her grandmother looked at her as if she'd lost all of her common sense. "Rita's sauces have more lumps than an old mattress, and Margo's are just as hopeless. She might be a gem at Great Grilling and Roasting to Perfection, but that woman can't even manage to whip up a cake from a box mix."

Emily could certainly relate, despite her grand-mother's patient attempts to teach her otherwise. "Then you'll have to postpone those classes until next semester."

Grandy looked as if she'd just been insulted. "I'll do no such thing," she argued.

"Okay, I'll find a substitute for you."

"Emily, you know I love you. But you're more lost in the kitchen than Forrest Gump at a Mensa meeting."

She had her there. "True," she admitted without an ounce of shame. "But I do have an MBA from Columbia. I believe that qualifies me at least to handle the administrative end of things for you until you're up and around again."

"You're supposed to be on holiday."

"I don't mind, Grandy." And she didn't, especially since her vacation was going to last a lot longer than she'd originally planned. Anything was better than wallowing in her own problems. "I want to do it. In fact, I'm going to insist." She gave her grandmother a stern look. "From where you're sitting, you aren't in a position to argue with me."

Grandy frowned.

Emily lifted one eyebrow in silent challenge.

Silence reined for a moment before Grandy let out a defeated sigh. "Oh, all right. You win. For now." She wagged her finger at Emily as if she were a naughty child. "But I want final approval so you don't hire any old Joe off the street who says he can cook."

"I can handle it."

"Call the agency in my address book and tell them exactly what we need. These are late-afternoon and evening classes, so there's bound to be a qualified instructor looking for a little pin money."

"I'll take care of it, Grandy," she said with practiced patience. She knew how important the school was to her grandmother, but just because she didn't know a saucepan from a sauté pan didn't mean she was a complete moron. "I know what to do."

"You'll have to sign them on to teach the entire course. And draw up a contract."

Emily drew in a long, steady breath and let it out slowly. "Yes, ma'am."

Before Grandy launched into more instructions, Drew returned. One look at his face had Emily tensing. Something was wrong. "What is it?"

"I just spoke to my captain," he said, focusing his attention on Grandy. "I'm sorry to have to tell you this, Mrs. Norris. There's been another fire."

5

EMILY'S HEART gave a sudden lurch when her grandmother's lashes fluttered closed. The moment her lips began to move silently, Emily knew Grandy was praying. Taking into account everything she'd been through recently, she didn't think a few prayers were particularly out of order.

She almost wished Drew had told her first so she could break the news to her grandmother herself, except Grandy did have a right to know her property had been damaged—again.

Grandy opened her eyes, now filled with moisture. "Please, tell me no one was hurt."

Drew shook his head. "Thankfully, no."

"There wouldn't be anyone at the school today," Emily reminded Grandy. "Not on a Saturday." She gripped her grandmother's hand and held it tightly, for her own comfort or her grandmother's, she couldn't rightly say. She looked up at Drew. "How bad was it?"

He tucked his hands in the front pockets of his trousers. "The damage wasn't to the school this time." He let out a sigh. "I wish I had better news, but the garage is gone. The crew responding managed to extinguish the flames before they spread to the house or school, so the damage has been contained to one structure. They weren't able to save the car, but arrived in time to prevent an explosion."

"Do you..." Grandy's voice cracked as she struggled to hold back tears. "Do you know how it happened?"

"I'm sure it's intentional, but I'll know more once I inspect the scene."

Grandy lay back against the stark white bed linens, looking frail and every second of her age. "I don't understand why this is happening," she whispered.

Neither did Emily, but she was determined to find the rat bastard and take whatever steps were necessary to ensure he spent the rest of his life behind bars.

"Grandy, is there anyone you suspect could be responsible?" She concentrated on keeping her voice gentle and soothing, a difficult task considering the dangerous combination of tension, fear and anger simmering inside her. "Someone with an ax to grind."

"Or a match to strike." Grandy bit out the words, her voice uncharacteristically hard. She winced, then let out a sigh. "No. Not that I can think of."

Drew moved from the foot of the bed. He settled his hand briefly over Grandy's shoulder, careful to avoid her injured arm and hand, in an unmistakable gesture of comfort. "I will stop whoever is doing this to you. You have my word."

Emily admired his determination, even if she hadn't a clue how he'd accomplish such a feat. Unless...

"I realize it's ridiculous even to say this," he continued as he pulled the chair up to the side of the bed and sat. "But try not to worry. Concentrate on getting well."

The slight curve of Grandy's brief smile was half-hearted at best. "Thank you."

Even Drew's promise to bring justice to the individual responsible failed to chase the worry from Emily's grandmother's eyes completely. Now, on top of some lunatic trying to destroy everything Grandy'd worked for over the past fifty years, the academy's best instructor would be laid up for who knew how long. Emily didn't mind assuming command, especially in such an emergency, but she wasn't about to stand idly by and let her grandmother be ruined by some wacko with a penchant for flames.

She thought about hiring a rent-a-cop to patrol the area, then quickly discarded the idea. Twenty-four-hour security didn't come cheap. Grandy's vehement refusal to cancel so much as two classes until she could teach them herself probably meant funding was an issue. While round-the-clock security might prevent another attack, scaring off the arsonist wouldn't lead to his or her capture.

The most logical plan of action would be to cancel all classes until Drew apprehended the culprit, but Emily had a feeling they'd be playing right into the arsonist's hands by doing so. No, what she needed was...

"Drew."

He'd think she'd finally lost it. Quite frankly, she thought so, too, but she refused to let that little detail stop her now that she'd latched onto her idea, and, she hoped, a solution.

"Yeah?"

"You need to catch this guy, right?"

"That's the idea."

She ignored the hint of sarcasm in his voice and plunged ahead before she lost her nerve. "I know how you can do it."

He leaned back in the chair, a patronizing expression on his face. "Oh? And how is that?"

"Substitute teaching."

"I'm not following you."

"By taking over Grandy's classes. They're in the evening so it wouldn't interfere with your other investigations. And, it'd give you an opportunity to observe some of the students and staff."

"Emily..." Grandy started.

"No," she interrupted. "He'd be perfect. He's a great cook."

Drew leaned forward, hands braced on his knees and spoke slowly. "Not a chance."

"Why not?" The idea made perfect sense to her. He was an arson inspector. There was an arsonist on the loose who could very well be a staff member or student of the school. These weren't random fires. Someone was specifically targeting her grandmother. "You know how to cook."

"That doesn't qualify me to teach," he argued. "This is the Norris Culinary Academy, not the Acme Truck-Driving School."

Her grandmother's expression grew thoughtful. "Is he really that good?" she asked Emily.

"I think so. And I bet your students will get what

they pay for. You have lesson plans, don't you, Grandy?"

"Yes, I do." Grandy smiled at her, then shifted her attention to Drew. "So, you have taught before?"

Drew shook his head, feeling as if he'd just followed the Mad Hatter down the rabbit's hole. "Not in the culinary arts," he told Velma before shifting his attention back to Emily and the determination in her big brown eyes. "And I don't get it. How do you expect me to catch an arsonist while whipping up a few cakes and pies?"

"That's my Down Home Delights course," Velma said. "More elaborate desserts like crème brûlée, cherries jubilee and baked Alaska are in line with Elegant Desserts."

"Simple," Emily said, as if it were just that. "If you're at the school as an instructor, you'd have the opportunity to observe the students and staff in an unofficial capacity. Kinda like an undercover fire cop."

Arson inspectors *were* known as fire cops, but last time he'd looked at his job description, *undercover* hadn't been listed.

He suspected his reluctance might have more to do with the matter of one incredibly hot kiss which refused to leave his mind. Passing off the incident as an unconscious action caused by her dreams of kissing another guy wouldn't fly, either. Not when she'd gone and murmured *his* name in her sleep as he'd tried to wake her. Oh no, she'd been kissing him all right, and he hadn't exactly been an unwilling participant.

She'd tasted good. So good he wouldn't mind a repeat performance. But there were other issues needing his attention, his self-preservation for one.

Not only had he spent the last twelve hours inside a hospital, he'd been continually plagued with visions of kissing Emily senseless. Spending more time with her than absolutely necessary was a definite concern. But he did have a firebug to catch, and she had made a good argument, one he couldn't ignore any more than he could forget the way her lips had tasted.

He'd just have to make damned certain he kept his priorities in line, which shouldn't be all that difficult since she wouldn't be in town for more than a few weeks. A detail which suited his short-term-relationships-only rule to perfection. The last thing he needed, or wanted, was a clingy woman falling for him in a way that made him uncomfortable.

"Okay." His imagination conjured a knight in armor, fighting a fire-breathing dragon. "I'll do it."

For safety reasons, he tried to convince himself. For Emily and the staff and students at the school. It really wasn't at all unusual for an arson inspector to spend extended periods of time at the scene of the crime, and since this particular firebug did appear to have it in for Velma or the school, Emily's crazy plan actually made sense. Spending more time with Emily didn't make sense.

Gratitude filled her gaze as she gave him a warm smile. "Thank you," she said.

His heart rate really shouldn't have increased simply because she'd smiled at him. The physiological acceleration couldn't be prevented any more than could the images of her body pressed against his.

"Well, that problem's solved," Velma said, her relief apparent in the way she settled back comfortably against the pillows. "One less worry."

Maybe for Velma. He had a bad feeling his had only just begun.

A rail-thin, older nurse bustled into the room. She tossed him and Emily a harsh look, enhanced by an angry scowl which deepened the heavy lines on her weathered face. The tightly wound bun of silver hair at the top of her head made her look even more stern.

Drew stood. Unlike his brother, he *could* take a hint. "We should be going so you can rest," he said to Velma.

The nurse muttered incoherently as she read the thermal graphs spewing from the monitor, then turned her scowl on Velma.

Emily rose in obvious preparation for battle if the crotchety nurse uttered so much as a single harsh word to Velma.

"Are you in pain, hon?"

In his line of work, not much surprised Drew, but his jaw fell open at the sound of the sweetest, most compassionate voice he'd ever heard.

"A little," Velma said.

"On a scale of one to ten?"

"Seven."

The nurse's mouth twisted into what looked more like a grimace than a smile. "We'll get you aboard the Morphine Express right away." She turned her grimace on Emily. "I'm on duty until eleven. You call me anytime to check on your grandmother."

"Uh...thank you," Emily stammered, obviously as shell-shocked as he. To Velma she said, "I'll come back in the morning, Grandy. Is there anything you need? Anything you need me to take care of for you at home?"

"The books need to go to the accountant Monday morning, but that's the only thing I can think of at the moment."

Emily leaned down to kiss her grandmother goodbye. "Don't worry," she said. "Everything will be okay, Grandy."

"It will, you know," he said once they exited Velma's room.

She looked up and gave him a wry smile. "I hope you're right," she said. "Because I hate offering false hope to the most important person in my life."

EMILY STOOD at the edge of the driveway behind a ribbon of yellow crime scene tape and stared in disbelief at the charred remains of the garage and what had once been a well-maintained, older-model Ford Taurus. The acrid scent of burned wood, smoke and chemicals permeated the air, causing her stomach to roll.

The roof had collapsed, but the footings remained, stretching nightmarishly toward the sky. Amid the rubble crouched Drew. He wore a pair of surgical gloves on his big hands, and had discarded his shovel for a small metal object which he used to gently lift the corner of some twisted object she couldn't identify from a distance. The damage was so extensive, she doubted she'd be able to recognize a single object from the garage if she held it in her hands.

She'd expected anger, but all she could summon was shocked disbelief that any one person could intentionally cause so much damage. Structures could be replaced. So could the car. The emotional aspect of the situation was an altogether different matter.

For all intents and purposes, someone was out to get her grandmother. Maybe not physically, but if the person responsible wasn't caught soon, Emily had to face the fact that her grandmother could very well end up with more than an injured arm.

By the time she and Drew had returned to the house, the firemen were long gone, but a pair of patrolmen lingered. They'd questioned her extensively, but the information she'd given them had been limited to the few facts she knew.

Drew had requested copies of the student files and employment records of the staff for himself, as well as the officers. While she'd gone into the office to make copies, he'd donned his gloves and begun rummaging through the charred skeleton of the garage. Since he'd still been digging around for clues when she'd finished with the copies, she'd gone into the house to take a hot shower and change clothes, then had returned to Grandy's office for a little research. A little over two hours later she'd seen more than enough to draw a few conclusions.

She left the coolness of the building's shade and ventured across the courtyard under the blistering heat of the late-afternoon sun. Drew continued to examine the damage. She crossed the driveway to the small patch of grass and sat cross-legged beneath the Spartan shade of the eucalyptus trees, careful to spread her floral silk skirt over her legs. She leaned back on her hands and kept her gaze on Drew as he worked.

Her mind wandered down an unfamiliar path. One that filled her with an aching sadness. As much as she would've preferred to bury her head in the sand, she couldn't ignore the truth. She'd harbored a few suspicions about the school suffering financially, and she'd been right in her assumption. In the past six months, her grandmother had scaled back, not just on the number of classes she taught, but the overall curriculum had been reduced by a third. After further review, Emily had surmised the decision stemmed more from the low enrollment numbers than from any need by her grandmother to slow down.

She'd already made the decision to extend her visit, at least until her grandmother was able to take care of herself again. She had no reason to return to New York to no job, no apartment and no father for her baby. Why couldn't Charlie have just been honest with her and admit he hadn't loved her? Was that so difficult?

For Charles Pruitt, III? Yes. The man had been taking the path of least resistance for as long as she'd known him. Why someone who despised personal conflict as much as he did had become an attorney was another mystery she'd never understand.

So, what exactly was she supposed to do now? She

might extend her stay in Los Angeles, but she couldn't very well live here forever.

Or could she?

At the moment, her grandmother needed her to see to the day-to-day running of the Norris Culinary Academy. When the doctor released Grandy from the hospital, Emily would be here to look after her. But once Grandy recovered, Emily would need a job and a place to live. By that time, her pregnancy would no doubt be showing, and her chances of finding an advertising firm willing to employ a woman preparing to take twelve to sixteen weeks of family leave within months of being hired were slim to none. She could always temp until after the baby was born, provided she found an agency that dealt with advertising executive placement.

She glanced up in time to see Drew walking toward her. Her concerns took a back seat as she stared, entranced by the way his shirt clung damply to his chest. As he neared, she spied rivulets of sweat running from his hairline. He stopped and crouched beside her. Using his biceps, he swiped at the sweat on his brow. Rumpled and sweaty from digging through the rubble under the stifling heat, he still managed to exude more than enough sex appeal to send her feminine senses into a frenzy of activity.

Her imagination took off like a racehorse at the first bell. Drew's sweat-slicked body moved over hers. His hands glided over her own moistened flesh, creating a heat wave inside her as he...

Cleared his throat?

A frown creased his brow. The green of his eyes darkened, making him appear cold and unapproachable. "Pack your things," he said in a tone filled with authority. "You're not staying here tonight."

She bristled, not appreciating his high-handedness in the least. With her hands still braced behind her on the grass, she casually unfolded her legs and stretched them out in front of her. "I'm not going anywhere." The thought of room service tempted her, but without gainful employment, she needed to be careful with her money.

He let out a rough sigh and shoved his hand through his windblown hair. "Emily," he said wearily, "don't argue with me. It's not safe for you to stay here alone."

She lifted her shoulder carelessly. "I'm not leaving, so you can forget it." She'd already been tossed out of one home. She'd be damned if she'd be booted from another—all in the same week.

"You need to understand that this is a serious situation. A few oily rags left lying near a faulty electrical outlet didn't cause this fire. Nor did a carelessly tossed match. This was an intentionally set blaze, and it's pure dumb luck the house or the school weren't taken, as well." He let out a sigh. "Emily, you need to close the school."

"I appreciate your concern, but I can't do that. I spoke to the two officers, and they're going to see to it that the area is patrolled."

"That's not good enough," he said roughly.

She lifted an eyebrow. "Well, it's just going to have to be. We can't afford to close down and I'm not leaving so some nutcase is free to torch everything my grandmother has ever worked for." She pulled her feet close and stood. "Thank you for your concern and for all you've done. Now, if you'll excuse me, I'll see you Monday evening."

She took off toward the house. She understood his concern, but since there'd been no loss of life and the building, insofar as building codes went, was not a hazard, the decision belonged to her. Ultimately, Grandy could close the school, but she'd made her opinion clear when she'd refused to cancel classes.

Okay, so the idea of being alone didn't exactly thrill her, but no way would she turn tail and run. She'd meant what she'd said. If she had to patrol the area herself, she'd do it. Maybe she'd even look for Pop's old varmint gun.

She stepped inside the coolness of the house. When she turned to close the door, she nearly crashed into Drew's imposing frame blocking her path. She tipped her head back and almost winced at the irritation and frustration simmering in his mesmerizing eyes.

"I take it from the look on your face that you're not here for a goodbye kiss," she said, annoyed by the husky tone in her voice.

His gaze dipped to her mouth, and she had the sudden urge to draw her tongue across her bottom lip. She had an idea what it was like to kiss him. Hot. Wild. And if her subconscious was telling the truth, wholly intoxicating. The idea of doing so again, especially while conscious, suddenly held dangerous, tempting appeal.

She took a step backward and looked away from him before she did something really stupid, like wreath her arms around his neck and pull him down for a steamy, demanding kiss, the kind destined to curl her toes and start her body revving with anticipation.

The door snapped closed. She glanced up, and for the space of a heartbeat, hoped he'd be on the other side of it.

No such luck.

As if she had any, anyway.

"You can't really believe staying here is going to make a difference?"

"Yes, I do," she told him, determined to keep her mind on the conversation and not on the way he continued to sneak peeks at her mouth. "If we hadn't been at the hospital today, then this might never have happened."

He glared at her. "You can't be serious."

She folded her arms and glared right back at him. "Very serious."

"I know a hell of a lot more about the characteristics of an arsonist than you do," he snapped at her. "And if you think for a second that you can prevent him from striking again, you're mistaken."

"Good," she said sarcastically. "Then maybe I'll catch the bastard in action."

In two long strides, he narrowed the space between them. His large, warm hands settled gently on her arms. Sparks shot through her and settled with pinpoint accuracy between her thighs.

"I'm not trying to be the bad guy here." His gaze

softened, causing her insides to melt at the concern banked within those green depths. "I'm worried about you, Em. Is that such a crime?"

No, she thought. *That* wasn't a crime. Good thing those cops weren't around, because if his thoughts were anywhere near as illicit as hers, they'd surely be arrested for lewd and lascivious conduct.

6

THE SHAKE, rattle and roll of the San Andreas Fault wouldn't have stopped Drew from taking the next fatal step toward real danger. The blame lay at Emily's feet. Never had he encountered such an exasperating, stubborn, sinfully sensual woman.

His conscience told him *no*. Walk away now and keep going until he'd gained enough distance not to be able to stare into her big brown eyes or admire the way her backside curved or how her breasts pressed against her lemon-colored sleeveless sweater with each breath she drew into her lungs. Even the warning that he was about to complicate his life failed to provide him with the willpower to walk away and never look back.

He slid his hands up her arms, over her exposed shoulders and the remaining distance to the nape of her slender neck. If she tasted anywhere near as sweet as she felt beneath his fingertips, he'd be a goner in no time flat.

What was it about this particular woman, he wondered. Why, out of all the women he'd dated—and there'd been plenty—was she the one to stir his protective instincts, to make him forget his cardinal rule of absolutely no involvement? He intentionally kept his affairs entanglement-free because he never wanted to be the cause of the kind of pain that accompanied emotional involvement.

He had to be losing his mind. In his opinion, ever since Emily Dugan had fainted at his feet, the question of his sanity had been seriously up for debate. A synapse or two had to be misfiring. Personal involvement wasn't his style. His relationships with women were always light and easy, absolutely no strings attached. With the exception of his family and Tilly, the avoidance of emotional entanglements was as second nature to him as breathing.

For the life of him, he had no easy answers. All he knew was that if he didn't taste her, his sanity would no longer be an issue.

He lightly pressed his thumb against the pulse throbbing at her throat. The beat was steady, sure and a hundred times less erratic than his own. He drew in a long, slow breath, taking in her fresh, clean scent, a lethal combination of tropical perfumed soap and soft femininity, capable of bringing him to his knees.

Her eyes darkened, the color reminding him of thunderclouds at midnight. Wild. Untamable. A power he deeply respected. A hypnotic, sensual power she effortlessly and unconsciously wielded over him in ways he'd never imagined possible.

He dipped his head, but stopped before his lips brushed against hers. There was no indecision on his part, nor, he suspected, on hers. Still, he hesitated, wanting to know with absolute certainty she would be a willing participant.

Seconds ticked by with each heavy beat of his heart. Her warm breath caressed his lips.

"This is a mistake," she whispered as her hands landed on his chest.

He waited for her to push him away. She didn't.

He shrugged carelessly, as if kissing her hadn't suddenly become more important than drawing his next breath. "What's life without a few mistakes along the way?"

Her generous mouth curved and her soft laughter made him smile. "Pretty darned boring."

With her gaze locked on his, she leaned in, then traced the tip of her tongue in an erotic path along his bottom lip. Heat shot south faster than an accelerant-induced out-of-control fire.

He gathered her in his arms and pulled her the remaining distance. His mouth captured hers, and he found heaven. Tongues tangled and mated insistently. Hands moved frantically, exploring with hurried impatience. Bodies heated to temperatures rivaling the week-long heatwave blanketing the city.

Need clawed his gut. The touch of her skin beneath his hands drove him to distraction. The taste of her mouth, along with the erotic silken glide of her tongue against his, fed the powerful hunger inside him.

His control took a dive. When she plastered her body against his, he hardly cared, and urged her even closer. The tips of her fingers moved enticingly over his arms, then before he could think, she urgently tugged his shirt from the waistband of his trousers. His testosterone level shot through the roof like the flames of a four-alarm blaze.

Conflicting sensations, the heat of her hands smoothing over his torso and the cool blast from the air-conditioning, only served to heighten the intensity of the spell she cast over him.

Blindly, he managed to guide them to the sofa where he gently followed her down onto the soft, overstuffed cushions. She clung to him, her lush, full breasts pressing intimately against his chest. Silently, he cursed her sweater. He wanted to be skin to skin. Breast to chest. Bared thigh to bared thigh.

Her hands moved over his body, each touch another stroke that had him leaving common sense behind and carried him closer to the brink of no return. Her fingers eased down his chest, until she slid her hand between their bodies and cupped his erection through his trousers. A barely detectable moan filled with need erupted, and he had no idea if he'd made the sound or if the erotic purr had come from Emily. He was almost past caring.

She shifted beneath him to hook her leg around his, holding his body intimately against hers despite the clothing separating them. When her hips rose to meet his in a silent old-as-time invitation, he groaned from the sweet, delicious agony of being unprepared to fulfill the natural culmination of their lovemaking. Contrary to his reputation, he didn't walk around with a pocketful of condoms.

With deep regret, he slipped his hand around her satiny-smooth calf and gently eased her leg onto the sofa. "Emily, we can't." The strain of his voice pierced the silence.

Her own pained expression matched the ache inside him. "We can't?"

"I'm sorry, honey." Using his elbows for support, he smoothed the hair from her face with his hands, then placed a quick, hard kiss on her lips. "You don't know how sorry I am, but I don't have any protection."

Her eyebrows rose. "It's not like you can knock me up, you know," she sassed, then winced the second the words left her mouth. "I apologize. That was a really bad thing to say."

He didn't care much for the reminder, either, but he'd never made a habit of avoiding the truth. He had a serious case of the hots, and he didn't think it'd matter if she were carrying a set of quadruplets. Heaven help him, he'd still want her.

He eased back to sit on the cushion. Instead of taking advantage of the distance between them to regain his composure and cool his libido, he foolishly lifted her slender ankles, slipped off her sandals and settled her feet across his lap. "Tell me about it."

Both of her eyebrows winged up in surprise. "About what? The baby?"

He shrugged. "The baby. The baby's father." Just because the guy dumped her, as she'd so indelicately phrased it, didn't mean he wouldn't walk back into her life when he came to his senses and realized what an incredible woman he'd let slip through his sorry fingers.

She lay back on the sofa and stared at him quietly for a few moments. "Are you for real?" she finally asked.

"What do you mean?"

"I mean," she said, her eyes filled with obvious confusion, "what planet are you from?"

He frowned, not sure if she'd just insulted him or not. "Excuse me?"

She adjusted the tapestry throw pillows behind her and settled back again. "I thought guys like you only existed on the silver screen. You know—make-believe, fiction, the unrealistic object of some silly romantic notion that fairy tales can happen."

Ah, a cynic after his own heart. "Why?" He took her foot in the palm of his hand and gently massaged the arch of her foot. "Because I'd like to learn more about you?"

"It's not just that. First you keep a promise to some goofball doctor who mistakenly thinks you're my husband. You not only stay the night when you obviously have so many other places to go, but then you go and hang out with me half the night and nearly all day in a hospital room with an old woman. If that's not enough to earn you some sort of medal of honor, you agree, albeit reluctantly, to teach gourmet cooking classes all while attempting to track down an arsonist."

Considering how much he detested hospitals, he hadn't been all that comfortable spending so much time in one, but in his opinion, she'd needed him, if only for silent emotional support.

The mythical white charger reared up, pawed the

air, then took off like a shot, leaving behind a cloud of dust...and confusion.

"Now," she continued, "you want to know about my baby, and even my baby's father. *After* we almost make love. When do I get to see the web shooting out of your palms so you can scale tall buildings in a single bound?"

"Superman does the tall building trick." Drew reserved his talents for foot massages. Among other things.

"Well, excuse me, Mr. Superhero, but those khakis aren't doing much to hide your blue tights."

"Maybe I'm just interested in a beautiful woman." It worked for him.

"I think it's an extremely inventive method of trying to score." The wry humor in her voice belied the wariness in her eyes.

The caution intrigued him. Hell, just about everything about Emily intrigued him. Which should have had him bolting for safety, not playing masseuse because he couldn't not touch her.

"Look," she said. "Even though my judgment when it comes to men is severely flawed, I really do think you're a nice guy. I just want to know if you're for real."

He hadn't been dealt the hero gene. Cale was the one with that complex. Even Ben played the role to perfection, but only when it came to the job. Neither Drew nor Ben was anywhere near as obsessed as Cale had once been. These days, his brother reserved his heroic talents for his future bride.

Drew shrugged. "I only agreed to take on the classes in hopes of nailing a firebug."

"And that's the only reason?"

"Should there be another one?"

The delicate arch of her brows rose a notch, as if she didn't believe him. Funny, he was having his own difficulties with the subject.

"I'm asking the questions here."

He settled her foot back onto his lap and lifted the other into his palm. "I'm not too thrilled about the teaching aspect, but you made a good argument. It could lead me to the arsonist. In this case, I didn't arrive on scene until after everyone had been sent home. There weren't any students or teachers at the school by the time I showed up. No one has seen me, so it just might work."

He enjoyed talking with her, holding an intelligent conversation. Not exactly a claim he could make about most of the women he dated.

He didn't want to discuss his investigation, primarily because he didn't relish telling her that whoever was setting fires had upped the stakes. He'd easily determined the cause of the garage fire, and while the cause wasn't particularly sophisticated, the arsonist had graduated from common vegetable oil to gasoline.

He had no idea if the school had been suffering financial difficulties, but he did have his suspicions on that score even if he had dismissed the idea that someone was setting the fires to cash in on the insurance, which effectively removed Velma from his list of possible suspects. He had his doubts about a garden-

variety pyromaniac, as well. The person responsible
for starting the fires had one goal, and in Drew's opinion, revenge for some perceived wrong stood out as
the strongest motivating factor.

He pressed his thumbs into the ball of her foot and
rotated them slowly.

"God, where'd you learn to do that?" Her lashes
fluttered closed and a soft moan of pleasure escaped
her lips, causing him agony.

"You sound like you're sorry you talked me into taking over those classes. What's the matter, Emily?" he
asked softly. "You don't like having me around?"

She opened one eye to a slit. "I don't care one way or
another just so long as you keep doing what you're doing."

"You never did answer my question."

She let out a sigh, but kept her eyes closed. "I
thought we were talking about you."

He ceased the foot massage, and after a moment, she
opened her eyes. "Hey," she said, pointing toward her
feet. "We're not done here."

He chuckled. "You want more, it's gonna cost you."

"Why do I have a feeling this is going to be one very
expensive foot massage?"

He smiled.

Her gaze narrowed with suspicion. "Ooh, for a superhero you don't play fair."

"Talk to me, Emily." The timer on the lamp clicked
on, chasing away the deepening shadows of early
dusk. "What happened to the baby's father?"

"Just one more in a long line of bad choices."

His curiosity climbed a notch. "Do you think he'll find being a parent will cramp his style?" Drew had known for years that fatherhood wasn't for him, which was why he never played without protection. Regardless of how careful he might be, accidents could still happen, but despite his own views on the subject, he'd never turn his back on his child.

"He doesn't exactly know yet, so I'm not sure," she answered slowly. "It's not like this was a planned pregnancy."

Which meant the guy could easily come back into her life when she told him they'd created a child together. "You do plan on telling him, right?" Something sharp pierced him. Jealousy?

Never. Not him.

"It's a little complicated," she said.

"Is he married?" Emily didn't strike him as the kind of woman to have an affair with a married man.

"No, of course not." She hesitated and bit her lower lip. "Well...he could be by now for all I know. He left me for another woman."

Ouch.

"I'd been working horrendous hours and came down with a wicked cold. I didn't have time to go see a doctor, so Charlie stocked me up on cold medications. I never for a minute thought about the effect they'd have on my birth control. Because of the hours I was putting in on the ad campaign, I figured it was just exhaustion and I was having a rough time bouncing back. When the flu, or what I thought was the flu, hit me, not once did I even consider that I might be pregnant."

"You are going to tell him, though."

Nice work, Drew. Next time you can hold the door open for her so she can rush back into the sorry S.O.B.'s arms.

She chewed her bottom lip again, then nodded. "I will. But not yet. Look, I know what you're thinking," she said defensively. "That I'm this horrible woman who's going to deprive her child of his natural father, but that's not even close. The guy dumped me. He'd been having an affair for months, and I didn't have a clue. If I tell him now, he's going to think this is some desperate attempt to get him back, and that's the last thing I want."

For reasons he didn't care to examine too closely, her revelation filled him with a hefty dose of relief. "What *do* you want?"

She shrugged her slender shoulders. "Don't know. The day before my vacation, I was laid off. Charlie informed me he's keeping the apartment. Technically I'm homeless and unemployed, and I have a child to think about now. Who knows how long my grandmother is going to be in the hospital? And when she's released, she's going to need someone here to help take care of her. Right now, I'm needed here. Besides, what reason do I have to go back to New York, anyway?"

He waited, but not a single warning signal alerted him to the problems that lay ahead. In fact, the notion of her remaining in California failed to generate an ounce of dread. That truth alone should have had him scooting out the door and outrunning his mysterious white charger.

"You could work for your grandmother until after the baby's born." He couldn't believe it. Since when did he encourage a woman to stick around? He'd always made it crystal clear that anything longer than a couple of weeks of fun and games was out of the question. "She's going to need someone to run things for a while and would probably feel better having a family member take over for her."

Emily stretched her arms over her head and gripped the sofa arm behind her. "I've thought about it, but the only thing I know about gourmet is the Budget kind you throw in the microwave. The administrative end of the business, no problem, for a while at least. But Grandy would be better off hiring someone more qualified in education administration. I'm an advertiser, not an educator, even though I have my doubts about finding gainful employment now."

"Discrimination is illegal."

"Big deal. It's not exactly ethical to accept a job knowing I'll be taking an extended leave of absence in a few months when the baby arrives, either."

"So you're planning to stay?" The answer shouldn't have held any more importance to him than the weather forecast, but in fact, the opposite was true. He only wished he could understand why.

"For the time being, I suppose, but I've yet to make any long-term decisions. So much has happened in the last couple of days, I haven't had time to absorb it all. I feel displaced, and I'm still trying to get used to the fact that I'm going to be someone's mother."

"Parenthood is a big responsibility to shoulder alone." Not that he had plans of applying for the job of her assistant, but he knew what it was like to grow up in a single-parent household.

She regarded him quizzically. "That part doesn't bother me."

"But something does," he prompted when her frown made a reappearance.

"Let's just say I'm grateful I had Grandy as a role model. My mother, and I use the term loosely, was never into that whole domestic scene."

"A woman can have a career and still be a good mother, Emily. Mine was a firefighter long before it was considered acceptable." And the job had cost her her life, leaving behind three sons and a husband who mourned the loss of his wife so deeply, it had killed him.

"Glynis worked, but at being a free spirit." An edge of bitterness filled her voice. "A lifestyle much easier to accomplish without a demanding daughter begging for her attention. My grandparents raised me for the most part. Whenever Glynis decided she wanted to play Mommy, it never lasted more than a couple of months, then I'd be sent back to live with Grandy and Pop."

Until now, he'd never actually thought of himself as sharing a common bond with anyone other than his brothers, or maybe Tilly. Like Emily, he'd been raised by someone other than his parents. At the time, he'd only been a little kid and hadn't realized the impact he and his brothers had had on Debbie's future, but at a young age, their aunt had shouldered the responsibility of raising her nephews without ever showing them a lick of resentment. She'd become mother, father and friend to each of them.

"I have an idea what it's like," he said, a little surprised by the admission. He'd never before spoken of his private life with a woman outside of the family. "My aunt raised me and my brothers after my folks died."

A sense of discomfort nudged him as compassion filled her eyes.

"I'm sorry," she said. "How old were you?"

"Eight by the time my aunt took us in. It couldn't have been easy for her. She was young, around your age, I guess, but I never heard her complain once."

A slight smile curved her mouth. "Your aunt sounds like a very special woman."

"She is." He looked at her thoughtfully for a moment. "She'd like you."

She rolled her eyes as she pulled her feet from his lap and swung them to the floor. "I bet you say that to all the girls." She stood and lifted her arms over her head and stretched. "It's all part of this whole charm thing you have going. Very effective, too, I might add."

He didn't like that she considered him a charmer, as if he were all show and no substance. "No," he said, standing. "I don't say that to all the girls."

Covering her mouth with her hands, she yawned.

Loudly. "Excuse me," she murmured. "It's been a really long day."

He took the hint. They still hadn't resolved the issue of her remaining in her grandmother's house...alone.

"Will you come with me," he asked, "or should I stay the night?"

She lifted her chin a notch, obviously preparing for another argument. "Neither." Her stubborn tone equaled the determination in her sleepy gaze. "I'll be fine."

The tight line of her lips made him want to kiss them until they were soft, pliant, welcoming. She looked so damned adorable when riled, he could easily stand around and argue with her all night, but the shadows beneath her eyes brought him to his senses. Keeping his hands to himself if he stayed with her would be next to impossible. He also had a few doubts about his ability to convince her she shouldn't be alone in the house.

He tugged his wallet from his hip pocket and withdrew a business card. "My cell phone number," he said, handing her the card. "You hear a single noise, you call. You get spooked, you call. You need me for any reason, you call."

She tucked the card between some wax fruit in a milk-white glass bowl on the maple coffee table. "There goes the superhero image. I thought you guys had supersonic hearing and X-ray vision."

If he wasn't dead serious, her sass might have amused him. Right now, it irked him. "Promise me, Emily."

She let out one of those little puffs of breath which spoke volumes. "Okay. Okay. I promise."

He wasn't completely satisfied, but what choice did he really have? He couldn't very well play caveman and toss her over his shoulder to carry her off to someplace safe.

"Oh, don't forget these," she called to him as he reached the door. "The files you wanted and Grandy's lesson plans. You'll need those for Monday."

He took the folders and tucked them under his arm. "What time did you plan to see your grandmother tomorrow?"

She reached around him and opened the door. "Around ten or so. Why?"

"I'll swing by and pick you up. I won't be able to stay, though, because I promised to pick up the cake for the wedding shower tomorrow, but I can come back for you in the afternoon."

"You're going to a bridal shower?" She offered a hint of a smile, just enough to draw his attention to the slight curve of her mouth. "Isn't that a ladies-only affair?"

"It's more of a party," he said as he slipped through the door. "I'll see you in the morning."

"That isn't necessary."

The click of the lock on the screen door echoed between them in the darkness. "In case you haven't noticed," he said, "your grandmother's car went up in smoke today. The hospital's nearly ten miles from here, and after what happened to you yesterday, it's not a good idea for you to walk around in this heat."

She slipped her hands in the side pockets of her skirt and leaned against the doorjamb again. "Compared to New York subways, RTD is a walk in the park. I grew up here, remember?"

Reluctantly, he stepped off the porch, shaking his head. "I'll see you Monday, then."

"Drew?"

Hopeful, he stopped and turned.

"Thank you," she said quietly. "For everything. I really do appreciate it."

He nodded, then took off toward his vehicle, his hopefulness changing to disappointment that she hadn't asked him to stay.

7

"YOU AGREED to do *what?*"

Why he'd gone and ruined a perfectly good Sunday evening celebrating with family and friends the upcoming nuptials of Cale and Amanda by answering Tilly's questions about Emily, Drew couldn't rightly say. He supposed his willingness to sing like the proverbial canary had more to do with the continuing question of his sanity rather than with any dire need to confide in his best friend.

Okay, so Tilly *had* asked him about Emily. She'd treated her in the ER. Maybe if he was in a more charitable mood, he might even be a little understanding of her curiosity. Tilly knew him better than anyone, maybe even his own family. When he hung around a hospital for not one, but two days in a row, with his intense dislike for hospitals, his behavior was bound to raise a few questions.

He propped his shoulder against the refrigerator door. "I've taught classes before," he said in defense. "I have an idea what I'm doing."

Tilly slipped a trio of miniature quiches onto her plate, paused, then added another. "Teaching basic arson detection to a classroom full of rookies at the fire hall is a far cry from showing somehow how to make pastries at culinary school," she reminded him. "I can see Cale helping some woman who's down on her luck, but you? You're not the one who has to rescue every stray that comes along. Cale is."

"Was," Drew corrected her. Cale had all but retired his superhero gear ever since Amanda had come into his life, at least as far as rescuing damsels in distress. The way Drew figured it, his future sister-in-law had fulfilled whatever void had been a part of Cale's psyche, eliminating the need for him to right the world around him. At least to some degree, anyway. Drew suspected that, like most people in his brother's line of work, Cale would eventually turn to instruction after a few more years as an active paramedic. The chances of him turning away a stray animal were minute, however. In fact, just last week Amanda had mentioned something about Cale adding another homeless kitten to their menagerie of pets.

Tilly slipped a chin-length lock of sable hair behind her ear. "Maybe you should come in for tests. I think you could be seriously ill."

He crossed his arms, not at all offended by her good-natured sarcasm. "Bite me, Tils."

"Something already has." She propped her backside against the counter and smiled. "Or someone. Emily Dugan perhaps?"

He definitely shouldn't have said a word to Tilly, especially since he sensed an all-out interrogation coming. He shrugged. "So? She's an attractive woman."

"With a brain, too," Tilly teased him. "I picked that

up from her right away. Productive gray matter is a vital element missing from your usual type."

"I've dated smart women before," he answered defensively. Well, some of the time.

He vainly attempted to recall a name...and came up empty-handed.

Tilly rolled her eyes, then popped a miniquiche into her mouth. "I have one word for you, Drew," she said after a moment. *"Bimbo.* And an understanding that red means stop and green means go isn't the equivalent of intellect. More like basic urban survival skills."

"Oh, like you've dated nothing but winners," he countered, remembering how Tilly had used his shoulder to cry on more than once in the past, whenever some loser wounded her pride. "Speaking of which, how's Scorch treating you?"

She dragged a tortilla chip through the spicy cheese dip on her plate. "Don't you dare get all big brother on me. I can handle Tom McDonough just fine on my own."

He didn't doubt her claim for a second. She'd been dating Scorch for the last couple of months, but both parties had been unusually silent in that regard, raising Drew's suspicions that their relationship was indeed serious. If Tilly was happy, that's all that mattered.

Laughter from the living room caught his attention and he glanced over his shoulder. Cale and Amanda sat together on his aunt's love seat surrounded by several gifts wrapped in varying shades appropriate for a bridal shower. Since the party guests consisted mainly of the crew from the firehouse and their significant others, most of the gifts were gags with a sexual bent, a long-standing tradition with the crew members of Trinity Station. They were reserving the more traditional wedding gifts for the wedding the following weekend. Even the cake Drew had picked up that morning for his aunt was non-traditional, bearing a caricature of a man running from a burning building with a redhead slung over his shoulder. The balloon caption over the woman's head read, "Who am I?"

Amanda blushed prettily as Cale held up a scrap of black lace in one hand and a large cardboard rendition of a Viagra prescription in the other, while his aunt snapped another picture.

Drew spied Scorch, lounging against the newel-post, a bottle of beer in his hand. He blamed Tilly for the miserable expression on his pal's heavily freckled face.

He turned to face her. "How long do you plan on making him suffer?" he asked her, referring to Scorch's admission of forgetting her birthday the previous week.

Her eyes narrowed slightly. "I haven't decided," she said as she reached for her wineglass on the counter beside her.

Poor Scorch, he thought, unable to stifle a grin. He'd known Tilly long enough to know firsthand she could be one stubborn woman. "Is it serious?"

"Dating is like shopping for shoes," she said airily. "You have to try on a few styles to find the right fit."

He wasn't buying her noncommittal response. "That's no answer."

"Well," she said, after devouring another miniquiche. "It's all you're going to get for the time being. Unless you tell me about Emily Dugan."

"You go first."

She laughed. "Nice try, pal, but I haven't fallen for that one since the fourth grade. What's going on, Drew?" The laughter faded, replaced by genuine concern. "I can't remember a time when you ever offered more than dinner and a movie—or a night of hot sex—to any woman."

Neither could he, for that matter. Maybe a kernel of truth did exist in Tilly's shoe analogy. He sure wouldn't walk into a store and buy a new pair of sneakers or work boots without trying them on first. Just because he'd gone above and beyond his standard operating procedure with the opposite sex this time, didn't necessarily mean Emily was the right fit, even if he did find her a whole lot more comfortable than his usual style.

Tilly exchanged her now-empty plate for her wineglass. She took a sip and peered at him quizzically over the rim. "She's different, isn't she?" she finally asked when he remained silent.

He shrugged as more laughter filled his aunt's house. How exactly did he explain his interest in Emily? Nothing about his behavior made sense, yet everything about her made perfect sense. Family had always been important to him and he respected her devotion to her grandmother. There was a deep inner strength about her he admired, even though her stubbornness frustrated him. Never had any woman he'd dated ever stood up to him the way Emily had done, but then again, he hadn't let one get close enough or hang around long enough to push his buttons before, either.

"Drew?"

He lifted his gaze to Tilly's, fearful of the answers attempting to take root in his mind. "Yeah," he reluctantly admitted. "She's different."

The admission made him edgy, unsettled. Until Emily, he'd always thought of women as an amusement, a source of entertainment...for brief periods of time.

Tilly took another sip of wine. "Is that such a bad thing?"

Hell yes, his conscience roared. He didn't get involved. His relationships, such as they were, remained short and sweet. Never had he allowed a woman to occupy his mind. Not in the way Emily had done.

"It'd never work," he said. The sharp stab of disappointment was as foreign to him as a second language.

"Why wouldn't it? Granted, I haven't spent all that much time with her, just when you brought her into the ER, but my first impression is that I liked her." She drained the last of her wine and set the glass on the counter beside her empty plate. "I can't say that about most of the airheads you bring around."

Speaking the truth had never been one of Tilly's failings. She could be brutally honest. Today was no exception.

Drew pushed off the refrigerator and moved to one of the bar stools at the breakfast bar and sat. "For one, she lives in New York City. Or she did," he corrected. "There's a chance she could end up moving to California."

Tilly shrugged. "That's not much of a problem as far as I can see, either way. They do have fires in need of investigating in New York, you know."

His family was here. He wasn't about to move three thousand miles away just to be with a woman. Not a chance. Of course, if she stayed, geography would hardly be an issue. "She's rebounding," he said, scrambling for more excuses.

Tilly folded her arms and gave him a look filled with a wealth of knowledge, the look that said she saw right through his flimsy arguments, as if they were nothing more substantial than the scrap piece of black lace Cale had held in his hands earlier.

"I hate to be the one to tell you this," she said, "but not all rebound relationships are destined for failure."

Was she referring to her and Scorch? Tilly had been on the rebound, so he'd understood why she'd put the paramedic through the wringer when he'd first shown interest in her. It'd taken her weeks to finally agree to go out with Scorch, not that Drew could blame her for being gun-shy in the relationship department. Not after discovering her previous boyfriend in bed with another woman.

"Yeah?" he questioned, not willing to give up the fight. For what? he wondered. His freedom? No way was he in danger of risking his bachelorhood. He was attracted to Emily. Big deal. He'd been attracted to a lot of women. "How about rebounding *and* pregnant?"

Tilly shrugged, then folded her arms. "And this is a problem because..."

"Because there's a father to her baby out there somewhere, and once she tells him about it, he might want her back. Okay, so the guy left her for another woman, but once Emily tells him he's going to be a father, that could all change. The responsibility of a child is involved here. Marriages have been based on a lot less, you know."

Tilly dropped her hands to her sides in exasperation. "For crying out loud, Drew. Has she said she wants to marry this guy?"

"Well...no," he admitted slowly. But she hadn't said she wouldn't, either.

"Just because she's going to have this guy's kid," Tilly argued, "doesn't mean she'll *want* to go back to him."

Maybe. Maybe not. Either way, it shouldn't matter to him in the least. He didn't get involved, dammit.

Tilly moved away from the counter and approached the breakfast bar. "You want to know what your problem is?" She leaned forward to rest her arms on the Formica top.

"No," he told her, primarily because he didn't like the direction their conversation had turned. "But I have a feeling you're going to tell me anyway."

"You're right," she said, determination filling her warm brown eyes. "You intentionally date women that are all wrong for you."

"I enjoy the women I date."

"Really? Then why don't you go out with any one of them more than a few times? Why hasn't anyone seen you with the same woman more than once?"

Because he didn't get involved. Because he preferred

to keep his relationships, such as they were, light and easy. No strings.

"Because they bore you to tears, Drew," Tilly said with more of that brutal honesty he was beginning to resent. "I don't think Emily does, and that has you more than a little nervous." She let out a sigh. "You're a sweet, funny, caring guy. Do yourself a favor. Get to know a woman you have something in common with for a change. You might find it's nowhere near as terrifying as you think."

Light and easy relationships, or safe and unemotional ones? his conscience taunted.

"You don't understand, Tils. It's not—"

"Yes, I do," she interrupted. "More than you think I do." She reached for him and cupped his face in her hands. "Drew, you are not your father."

Anger pierced him and he pulled away from her. She'd hit a nerve, and they both knew it. "I never said I was." The words erupted more coldly than he intended.

"Then tell me why you're so afraid to let a woman get close to you?"

He shot off the bar stool. "This conversation is over." To emphasize his point, he grabbed a cold bottle of cola from the fridge and headed out the sliding-glass door to the covered patio.

Instantaneous heat slammed into him, exacerbating his flash of temper. He'd been six when his mother had died, but he'd been old enough to know his old man had slunk into the bottom of a gin bottle and had never come out again. Alex Perry had given up when he'd lost his wife—on his family, on his career, and eventually, on his life. He hadn't committed suicide, but he might as well have. Instead, he'd lingered, allowing his forgotten sons to witness his slow demise.

Drew stood at the edge of the patio, allowing his temper to simmer. With the plastic bottle of innocuous cola clutched tightly in his hand, he stared into the darkness of the backyard where he'd played as a kid with his brothers and Tilly. Beneath the light of the full moon, he could see his aunt's vegetable garden needed watering. The sound of the sliding-glass door opening and closing along the track behind him drew his attention.

"You're not going to let this drop, are you?" he asked when Tilly came up beside him.

"I want you to be happy," she said quietly. "I care about you. You know that."

He lifted the bottle to his lips and took a long pull. The cool liquid did zilch to calm the rioting in his gut. "Then leave it alone," he said after draining nearly half the bottle.

"Tell me why, Drew." Her tone was a far cry from gentle and coaxing, but demanding and insistent instead.

He muttered a vile curse and turned to face her, knowing from years of friendship she'd hound him relentlessly until she wrangled the answer from him. "Because there's no way in hell I'm going to be the cause of the kind of suffering my old man went through after Mom died. When he lost her, it killed him, Tilly. You know that as well as I do."

Her eyes rounded in surprise as she absorbed his statement. "So," she said thoughtfully, "this has nothing to do with *you* getting hurt, but it's about you hurting someone else?"

He'd stunned her. Hell, he'd shocked himself by verbalizing the truth. The anger he'd been nursing started to ebb. "I refuse to be responsible for that kind of pain," he said in a softer tone.

She let out a long, even breath, tucked her hands into the front pockets of her olive-green walking shorts and rocked back on her heels. "You know what?" she said after a few moments of blessed silence. "I love you, Drew. You're my oldest and closest friend, but you're a moron."

He turned to look down at her. "Excuse me?" He expected one of her smiles, but instead found her glaring at him, her expression grim.

"You heard me."

"Now, wait just a minute—"

She put up her hand, effectively stilling his argument to the contrary. "You're an idiot. No wonder you're afraid of Emily. She's smarter than you."

"Are you finished yet?" he groused at her. He'd certainly had more than enough of Tilly's brand of psychoanalysis for one night.

Her expression held tempered disgust. She walked away from him, but stopped and spun around to face him once she reached the door. "You cannot control how someone loves you." She flung the words at him. They landed like blunt weapons against his conscience. "It simply is *not* your responsibility. And you'd better figure that out in a hurry before you compound your idiocy by letting Emily Dugan slip through your fingers."

"What makes you think I care one way or another?" He didn't, he tried to tell himself, but the words were too false and hollow to be anything but another emotional avoidance tactic.

A wry smile curved Tilly's mouth. "Denial," she said with a hefty dose of smugness that managed to spike his irritation again. "And if you didn't care, then we wouldn't be arguing, now would we?"

He looked away and downed the last of his soda. Because he didn't want to face the truth in Tilly's eyes? Or because he feared facing another kind of truth? The kind that forced the seam of his heart to open ever so slightly, just enough for someone to sneak inside when he wasn't looking.

Someone like Emily, with her big brown eyes, sassy mouth and a body worthy of worship.

Which could only mean one thing...she already meant more to him than he was prepared to accept.

Maybe, he admitted silently as his cell phone vibrated in his pocket. *Maybe*.

He slipped the cell from his hip pocket, and checked the caller ID. The LCD display indicated an out-of-area caller, which could mean just about anything. Since he was off duty, he considered ignoring the call and allowing his voice mail to collect the message, then quickly decided against it in case it was Emily.

Tilly disappeared into the house, allowing him privacy. "Yeah?" he barked into the phone, his emotions still raw thanks to Tilly's unique ability to make him look hard at himself.

"Drew?"

The relief in Emily's sweet voice put his protective instincts on alert and had his heart thudding. "What's wrong?"

"Nothing. Well, not nothing, exactly." She sighed heavily, then continued in a rush. "I'm lost. Not lost really. I know where I am. I took the wrong bus transfer. I'm not in a very good neighborhood."

Alarm skidded along his spine, effectively extinguishing the anger and frustration he'd been harboring only moments ago. "Where are you?"

"Grauman's Chinese Theatre." She let out another exasperated breath. "It's Sunday and the buses stop running early. I'm sorry to call you like this, but I didn't know what else to do."

Hollywood Boulevard after dark could be quite the interesting locale, filled to overflowing with a colorful cast of characters, from tourists to local street people, but it was no place for a woman to find herself alone at night.

He mentally calculated the distance from Santa Monica and factored in traffic. "Give me thirty minutes."

Her relief was palpable. "Thank you. I'll be in the outdoor complex. No way am I'm going to hang out near the curb again."

He frowned. "The curb?"

"I was hoping to hail a cab and ended up with a

proposition from a fat bald guy looking for a good time instead," she said, her voice tinged with humor.

Despite his concern for her safety, he still chuckled at her wit. "I'm on my way, sweetheart," he said, already heading for the house to say his goodbyes.

"Thank you," she said again, then disconnected the call.

As he slipped the phone back into his pocket, he wondered if a guy could suffer saddle sores from riding an imaginary white stallion.

8

As DARKNESS settled over the city, Emily watched in amusement as the streets of Tinseltown transformed into a virtual wonderland in their own right. An eclectic mix of street performers pandered for cash from soft-hearted tourists, while curious passersby gawked and stared in awe or stunned disbelief at the local color that ranged from twenty-dollar hookers to uniformed cops walking a beat in hopes of maintaining order.

Although the presence of street people had been toned down somewhat since the construction of the new Hollywood and Highland project, the night life on Hollywood Boulevard still ranged from the innocent to the illicit, from garish to glitz, all within a matter of a few feet.

More wilted than the dried-out begonias in Grandy's planter, Emily slumped against the wall beneath the ornate copper roof of the theater, near the concrete slab of Liz Taylor's footprints, to wait for Drew. She'd hated having to call him, especially after she'd made a point of informing him she'd have no trouble negotiating L.A.'s Transit District. She wouldn't have had a problem, either, if she'd been paying attention instead of daydreaming about him in the first place. The only reason she'd gotten off the bus near Grauman's Chinese

Theatre had been because of the familiarity of the historic Hollywood landmark.

She'd left the house that morning to spend the day with her grandmother, armed with a mystery novel, a bottle of water and a lightweight sweater to ward off the chill from the hospital's air-conditioning unit. Now, her feet ached—thanks to a new pair of sandals she hadn't thought to properly break in before hoofing it around Southern California—and her denim-blue sleeveless blouse and supposedly loose-fitting carpenter jeans clung to her sweat-moistened skin, adding to her discomfort. The fact she hadn't slept more than a few hours did little to improve her mood.

She blamed herself for her aching feet, faulted the weather for the sticky clothes and cursed Drew for her lack of sleep.

Under normal circumstances, she was a relatively deep sleeper and rarely, if ever, had difficulty falling asleep. But last night, whenever she'd closed her eyes, her imagination had fired up and burned hot, making slumber all but impossible.

Well, not exactly her imagination, she silently corrected. More like a continuous replay of that toe-curling, breath-stealing, promise-of-heaven kiss. It hadn't taken much for her to recall the erotic sensation of his hands gliding over her body, either. Nor had it helped matters that even now she could still feel the texture of his skin on her fingertips. And how could she possibly forget the intense electricity charging through her body when he'd pulled her so close that all that had separated them were the clothes she'd have willingly shed. If he hadn't come to his senses first, of course.

A blushing virgin she was not. Her list of former lovers might not rival those of some of her friends, but she'd had her fair share, even if they were dumb choices. What bothered her, however, was her inability to recall ever being swept so close to the edge by nothing more than a toe-curling, breath-stealing, promise-of-heaven kiss.

The man definitely had cornered the market in that regard, too. Just the thought of his seductive mouth made her sigh and had gooseflesh prickling her skin, despite triple-digit temperatures.

She didn't want to think about his awesome foot-massage skills any more than she cared to be reminded of her behavior, but doing either was equally hopeless. She'd never had a foot massage before. Unless the porn-film guy's totally bizarre foot-licking fetish counted.

Even with the creepy glimmer of her pitiful sexual history, she clearly understood she'd already become a willing victim to Drew's sensual spell. How could she not when the man kissed her like he'd meant it, *and* gave her a foot massage in the bargain?

Drew was such bad news for her. Didn't she have enough problems and life-altering decisions ahead of her without compounding matters by becoming involved with the guy? Not just any guy, either, but one who had dozens of women throwing themselves at him, or leaving messages on his cell phone voice mail. Thirteen of them, in fact.

Okay, so she'd *literally* fallen at his feet. That hardly meant she hoped to be the latest entry in his little black book.

A pair of women wearing too much makeup and outlandish big-hair wigs strolled past in five-inch platform heels and miniskirts that defied modesty. Emily picked up her backpack and slung it over her shoulder, moving deeper into the forecourt near Natalie Wood's and Jane Wyman's tiles.

Did Drew use a star system? she wondered. Or did he utilize some other method of categorizing the legions of females clamoring for his attention. "Probably," she muttered to herself, wondering if he used one star for the girls who always said no. Two stars probably indicated a woman suitable to accompany him to a company or family function.

She'd always thought of herself as a two-star kind of woman. Until last night. Maybe she'd qualify as a three-star mama, in a league with those for-a-good-time-call types. Or perhaps she'd sprung right to the top. Emily Dugan: four stars. Fast. Easy. A home run every time at bat.

She frowned. Definitely four stars. They hadn't actually made love, but if Drew hadn't stopped them, she'd have been cheering him on as he slammed that sucker over the fence and out of the park.

She kept her eye on the traffic, searching for Drew's big black SUV. Faulting her hormones for her outrageous behavior was as good an excuse as any, she supposed. Or maybe she'd plastered herself all over him like a sex-starved feline because she hadn't been laid in weeks. Eight of them to be exact.

That thought hardly elevated her mood. Not when she could no longer deny the truth. Try as she might, not a single, solitary excuse existed capable of chasing away the sinking feeling in the pit of her stomach that her reaction to Drew stemmed from her being severely attracted to him. To further complicate her already complicated life, she couldn't help but believe that Drew just might be the genuine article. A living, breathing sexier-than-any-man-had-a-right-to-be nice guy.

Even her customary cynical conviction that given time, he would turn out to be one more in a long line of bad choices, failed to alleviate her suspicions about Drew's character.

As she'd told her grandmother today during their visit, life never turned out the way you thought it should. Her five-year plan had been shot to hell by corporate downsizing, an unfaithful live-in lover and an unexpected pregnancy.

Maybe it was just that her life wasn't supposed to turn out the way she'd hoped. There had to be a universal rule on that very subject, probably etched in stone and definitely written into the fine print of her own personal karma account. An account grossly overdrawn.

Just as she considered playing tourist by comparing the size of her feet to Jane Wyman's, Drew entered her line of vision. Her heart lifted considerably as he walked purposely toward her. She told herself she was too exhausted to care, that she was merely thrilled to see him so he could escort her exhausted body home and nothing more.

The lie fell far short of convincing. Her happiness stemmed from one source—the sight of Drew excited her, period.

His forehead creased and concern lit his eyes. "Are you okay?"

"Fine," she said, smiling up at him. She slung her backpack higher on her shoulder. "Tired, but fine." *Now that you're here,* she silently added.

He took the backpack from her. "Let's get you home," he said gently, lacing his fingers with hers.

The acceleration of her pulse hardly surprised her. The comforting warmth of his hand clasping hers no longer confused her. She couldn't fault hormonal imbalance for her physical and emotional reactions to Drew. No, the blame lay in an irresistible attraction to him, in the electrifying chemistry that sizzled between them and in an overwhelming desire for a sweet-talking charmer who'd no doubt break her heart if she gave him half a chance.

Only one question remained: exactly how far was she prepared to go in exploring all that attraction, chemistry and desire?

Easy, she thought. *Straight to heaven and back again.*

THREE DAYS LATER, Drew hadn't unearthed a single lead in regard to the capture of the Norris Culinary Academy arsonist. He'd casually spoken to Margo and Rita, the only instructors employed during the late-summer session. Given the circumstances, he'd exercised caution so neither of them would become suspicious of his questions, but so far, neither woman had exhibited anything but the appropriate level of concern for Velma and the general safety of everyone at the school.

Monday night after his classes, he'd taken home copies of the files Emily had provided him, studied past and present employee and student records, and found nothing to raise a single red flag. He'd even recruited the assistance of Dave Byrd, another fire cop, to conduct physical interviews of the surrounding business owners, but the task hadn't turned up a shred of new evidence. To date, not even the crime lab had managed to garner a single lead.

Unless Drew wanted to blow his "cover," Dave would have to be the one to officially interrogate the other two instructors. Somehow, he'd figure a way to be present for those meetings.

Since the garage fire, there'd been no further incidents, but Drew still didn't like the idea of Emily being alone with the firebug at large. In his experience, since either Velma or the school seemed to be the prime target, he knew it would only be a matter of time before the arsonist struck again.

He stowed the last of the equipment and utensils from his Wednesday-evening class, shut down the classroom, then walked down the deserted corridor toward Velma's office where Emily waited for him. It'd take a team of Clydesdales to drag it out of him, but he actually enjoyed teaching something other than basic arson detection. His two classes were small, the students responsive and it didn't interfere with his job. Of course, there was the Emily factor to consider, a definite added bonus.

Since the night of his argument with Tilly, he'd become aware of a shift in his relationship with Emily. Not that they actually *had* a relationship, at least not in the "lover" sense, although the chemistry between them was all but combustible and increasingly impossible to ignore. His interest in a woman had finally extended beyond sexual into foreign territory—friendship.

Not once had he so much as kissed Emily in the last few days. That didn't mean the need burning inside him to taste her lips again had subsided, or that they hadn't come dangerously close. In fact, just the opposite. She had him twisted in knots with wanting her, but as he'd admitted to Tilly, Emily *was* different from the other women in his life. Taking the time to learn more about her had been a novel concept, but one he found himself enjoying. So much he'd turned down a couple of dinner invitations. His relationship with Emily would eventually move to the next inevitable level. In the meantime, he'd been the perfect, if frustrated, gentleman.

Moving slowly had its advantages, he realized, but the confusion and desire in her eyes whenever he backed off was nothing short of pure torture, and it was killing him.

He'd made a decision. Tonight he planned to take the first step toward that inevitable level.

As he neared Velma's office, the sound of Emily's voice reached him, and she sounded none too happy. Curious, he approached the room, stopping in the open doorway. With the cordless phone pressed against her ear, she paced the length in front of Velma's desk, her expression filled with anger.

The flowing skirt and cotton blouse she'd been wearing when he'd arrived had been exchanged for a pair of denim shorts and a white T-shirt with a red slash emblazoned across the front that made it look as if she'd run into a paint brush. Her flip-flop sandals slapped against the asphalt tile as she paced.

She stopped when she saw him and waved him into the room. "No, I'm staying in California," she said into the phone.

He propped his backside on the edge of the desk. The revelation of her decision to relocate hardly came as a surprise. Just last night she'd told him about a promising interview she'd had scheduled for that morning with an advertising firm in Venice Beach. Two days ago, she'd contacted an executive search firm in hopes of landing piecework, which would provide her with income and allow her the time necessary to oversee the running of the culinary academy until her grandmother recovered from her injuries.

She clenched and unclenched her fist. "Yes, I do have a job, not that it's your business any longer."

The temp agency had called her in a matter of hours with the name of a firm looking for someone to handle their overflow advertising on project-by-project basis.

From Emily's end of the conversation, it sounded to him as if she'd been offered the position.

Fire blazed in her eyes suddenly. "Of course I'm keeping the baby!"

Curiosity fled and was replaced by discomfort that increased by the second as he realized exactly whom she was speaking to—none other than the father of her baby. Not wanting to further intrude on a very private conversation, he stood to leave. Emily nailed him with her heated gaze and pointed her finger at him to stay, all but daring him to attempt an escape.

"I didn't call to argue with you." The heat in her voice matched the fury simmering in her eyes. "I'm having a baby. It's yours. Foolish me, I figured you'd want to know about it."

She pulled a handful of pens from the cup holder on the desk, then brutally jammed them back inside. "Of course I'm sure. *I* wasn't the one screwing around, remember?"

Her mouth tightened into a grim line as she listened to whatever line her ex fed her. She made that huffing sound which usually indicated her displeasure.

"Do you have a clue how narcissistic you sound? Not everything is about you, Charlie. This is about a baby." Her voice rose with each subsequent word. "A baby you and I created."

Listening again, she started tapping her foot impatiently. "Nothing," she said vehemently. "There isn't a thing I want from you."

Her mouth fell open, and her eyes widened. "I figured as the father, you had a right to know," she finally said after her moment of stunned silence. "What you do with that information is up to you."

She yanked the phone away from her ear, then jammed her finger against the end call button so hard, the phone slipped from her hands and clattered to the floor. Not that he could blame her for expressing a bit of temper. From what he'd heard, her ex hadn't taken the news of his impending fatherhood well.

"Bastard." She stooped to pick up the cordless, then set the phone on the desk with an abrupt snap. "Solid proof that my taste in men is not to be trusted. If I wasn't pregnant, I'd join a convent to save me from myself."

The image of Emily and all those lush curves hidden beneath a nun's habit was an act of sin in itself. She had a body made for worship, but definitely not the Hail Mary kind.

She drew in a deep breath, let it out slowly, then repeated the process—three more times. "I'm sorry," she said, her voice a tad calmer. "I shouldn't have forced you to sit through that."

Drew cleared his throat. "Don't sweat it." True, he'd been uncomfortable, but he'd stayed because to him, Emily had needed the moral support.

The barest hint of a reluctant, appreciative smile tipped one corner of her mouth. "I don't know why I decided to call Charlie tonight. I probably should've waited, but I wanted..." She paused, as if searching for the right words. "I wanted it settled between us. Was that so wrong?"

"No," he told her. He understood her motivation

completely. Her life had been thrown into a tailspin and from his own observations of her take-charge attitude in dealing with the students and staff of the school when they'd expressed concern about the fires and Velma's absence, she wasn't the kind of person to wander aimlessly. Life didn't happen to Emily Dugan. She made life happen for her.

She rolled her head from side to side, then pulled in another deep breath. "Maybe I should've waited."

He reached for her and carefully turned her so her back faced him. "Waited until when?" he asked. He settled his hands on her tense shoulders and rubbed gently. "Until after the baby's born? The longer you waited to tell him, the harder it would've been. You did the right thing, Emily. Like you said, the rest is up to him."

She let out a long pleasure-filled sigh and tipped her head forward. Her ponytail fell over her shoulder. The urge to press his mouth against the exposed flesh of her nape gripped him hard. The sheer agony of touching her strengthened his resolve to move their relationship to the next level.

Tonight!

Based on the one-sided conversation he'd been privy to, interference from Charlie Pruitt had just become a nonissue. Since she'd landed work, the threat of her returning to New York no longer existed, either. The only remaining obstacle in his way belonged solely to himself and how much he was prepared to risk.

He pressed his thumbs against the base of her skull and rubbed. "Can I ask you a question?"

"Hmm," she murmured. "Keep this up and I'll hand over the combination to the safe at Fort Knox."

"After the dust settles, Pruitt might decide he wants to be a part of your life again. Then what?"

She snapped her head up and looked over her shoulder at him. Her big brown eyes filled with an intensity that made him decide to tread with caution. "Then what? *Nothing.*"

He dropped his hands to his sides. "You obviously gave the guy one hell of a shock tonight, Em. Once he has time to think about it..." He shrugged, leaving the words unspoken. If some woman from his past came forward with news like the kind Emily had delivered to Pruitt, he honestly couldn't predict his initial reaction. Once he'd had time to absorb the information and think rationally, he didn't doubt for a minute that responsibility would be his number-one priority.

She turned and faced him fully. "Charlie and I are ancient *history*," she said earnestly. "We were probably over for a while, I just didn't take the time to see it."

"Come on, Em," he scoffed. "If he hadn't told you he'd been having an affair, you'd be on your way back to New York once your vacation ended. You were living with the guy. Where I come from, that spells serious relationship."

"I'm not in love with Charlie. I'm..." Her voice trailed off and she looked away, but not before he caught the softening of her expression.

I'm, what? In love with him? No, he wasn't arrogant enough to believe that's what she'd been about to say.

Inconceivable.

They'd only known each other a few days. All they had going was an acute case of undeniable attraction and sexual chemistry. A fact driven home by the way she constantly invaded his fantasies, especially at night when he was alone in his condo. Or in bed. Or during a cold shower he usually blamed on her. Hell, even when he made coffee in the morning, he couldn't stop thinking about her.

Okay, so he cared for her. He worried about her being alone at Velma's, but that didn't mean...

He'd fallen for her? *Impossible.*

So what if she crept into his thoughts when he least expected to find her there. Big deal. Sure, he wanted her, wanted her with a need so desperate it drove him to distraction. But love? Not a chance.

"If I'd been in love with Charlie," she continued, "he never would've gone looking elsewhere for what I couldn't give him. I cared about him. We were comfortable together, but that's not love."

"But you were hurt and pretty angry just a couple days ago," he argued. For his own self-preservation?

You bet, pal.

"Sure I was hurt, but only because I'd trusted him and he'd made a fool of me, not because he broke my heart." She let out a sigh. "He couldn't break something that never really belonged to him."

He didn't know how he was supposed to feel about that little insight. Surely not relief. But how else did he explain the sudden buoyancy lifting his heart enough to lodge it in his throat?

A tiny frown creased her forehead. "Have you ever been in love?" she asked him.

Incapable of speech, he shook his head in denial. Fear did that to a guy.

She folded her arms and tilted her hip to the side, brushing the inside of his thigh. "I once asked my mother why she divorced my father. She told me it was because she could imagine her life without him. As flakey as Glynis is most of the time, what she said made sense to me."

"Made sense how?" But he knew. Heaven help him, he knew.

"She told me that to know if you're really, truly in love, then try to imagine your life without that person in it. If you can, without any hesitation whatsoever, then you're definitely not in love." A slow, sinful smile curved her mouth as she eased her arms around his neck. "But," she continued, "if just the thought of *not* having that person in your life leaves you with a deep sense of emptiness, like there's a vital part of you missing, then without a doubt, you're in love."

He settled his hands on her hips and drew her close enough so their bodies touched. Not even her warmth could chase away the stark, cold fear climbing up his spine.

He didn't close his eyes. He didn't need to, because no matter how much he wished otherwise, he knew he'd never conjure another image of his life without Emily.

9

BY THE TIME they closed the school and walked across the courtyard to the house twenty minutes later, Emily knew something was different. Either her Drew-barometer had faltered completely, or some other indefinable element in their quasi relationship had been altered without her knowledge. A long overdue change, too, in her opinion. She hadn't picked up on a single, solitary vibe all night that he planned to execute what she'd come to think of as his method of operation—the Dump and Run.

For the past two evenings following his final class, he'd walk her to her door. Monday he'd left claiming he wanted to read files she had given him. Last night they'd sat on the brick steps of the porch and talked, sharing anecdotes of their youth, family and careers, enjoying the sultry warmth of the evening while the air sizzled between them, and he hadn't so much as tried to kiss her.

Frustration dogged her heels, primarily because she knew clear down to her toes that he wanted to kiss her. Her feminine radar was running in full-alert mode, but he'd done his best to extinguish her simmering lust by pulling the platonic routine. After their conversation, he'd smoothed his hand down her arm, held her fingers in the warmth of his palm for exactly two heart-beats, then ushered her into the house—with him remaining on the wrong side of the screen door.

Tonight, finally, she'd sensed a blessed, past-due difference and had been thrilled when he'd accepted her invitation for a slice of cheesecake. Tonight was the night. Tonight *had* to be the night. Not only was her grandmother scheduled for release from the hospital tomorrow morning, but with the arrangements she'd made for a home health-care provider to assist in Grandy's care, she'd effectively eliminated any hope of privacy.

She cut two thick slices of the white-chocolate–raspberry cheesecake she'd bought after her appointment with her new obstetrician that afternoon. During her visit with Grandy two days ago, and a full-out confession of her status as mother-to-be, her grandmother had urged her to stop by the nursery and ask one of the pediatric nurses on duty for a list of OBs in the area. After a few phone calls, she'd lucked into an appointment on Wednesday due to a cancellation.

Other than a minor lecture about informing Cheatin' Charlie of his newly acquired status as father-to-be, Grandy had been fully supportive of her decision to keep and raise her child alone. Not only was she thrilled over the prospect of a new great-grandchild to spoil, but when Emily informed her she'd be remaining in California, Grandy had practically shed tears of joy. Although she had encouraged Emily to move in with her permanently, Emily declined. Since she'd already landed a freelance position with one advertising

firm, her confidence in finding more firms willing to offer piecework grew. With her savings and moderate in-
vestment portfolio as a safety net, looking for a small,
affordable house nearby suddenly made a whole lot of
sense.

When Emily finally had her appointment, she'd
taken a trip to the drugstore for cocoa butter—to keep
stretch marks to a minimum, she hoped—and prenatal
vitamins. On her way out she'd spied a bakery across
the street. Unable to resist the tantalizing aroma of
fresh baked goods, she'd gone inside and suffered her
first official clichéd pregnant-woman craving. Warm,
just glazed doughnuts and a whole white-chocolate–
raspberry cheesecake. Life just didn't get much better,
or caloric, than that.

"What are your plans for Saturday?" Drew asked
suddenly.

She eased the first slice of cheesecake onto the plate
and shrugged. "Nothing really. I don't have to work,
since the meeting to discuss my first freelance project
for the ad agency isn't until next week. Why?"

He cleared his throat and shifted his weight from
one foot to another. She peered up at him, surprised by
his nervousness. Drew? The last of the red-hot, sweet-
talking charmers, nervous? A man with legions of females waiting to be his beck-and-call girls, anxious
about asking a woman for a date?

The ice surrounding her heart after her disastrous
phone call with Charlie began to melt slowly, effectively evaporating the remnants of her earlier tension.

"I have to...I'll be..." he stammered, then cleared his

throat again. "My brother..." He shifted his weight once more, too.

She slipped another slice of cheesecake onto the second waiting plate. "Have to what?" she prodded him ever so gently.

"My brother's wedding is Saturday," he blurted. "Would you go with me?"

And pass up a golden opportunity? The chance to spend quality time with Drew in the ultimate romantic setting? Not on his life. Especially now that she had regained a modicum of control over her own little corner of the world. Her only loose end had been Charlie, and she'd resolved that issue tonight with one phone call.

She still couldn't believe the lying dog had asked if the baby was even his. What was the saying about accusers with a guilty conscience? Obviously, Charlie suffered with one monster guilt complex if he dared to accuse *her* of sleeping around.

But now a precious life grew inside her, and suddenly everything about the changes in her life made perfect sense. A baby. *Her* baby, a detail Charlie had made abundantly clear during their heated exchange.

She pulled forks from the silverware drawer. "I'd love to," she said as casually as possible, given the silly excitement coursing through her body just because he'd formally asked her out on a date, one that included meeting his family. Although she couldn't help wondering if his asking her meant she'd been demoted from four to two stars.

Not that it mattered. She was hardly in the market for forever, especially with someone as commitment-phobic as Drew. But that didn't mean she wasn't free to enjoy his company while it lasted. Maybe she'd even start her own little *pink* book. Drew could have the honor of being her first entry. With four *lips* beside his name.

He let out a rush of breath filled with such obvious relief, she smiled. "The wedding's at six, but Ben's picking me up around three so we can have Cale at the church on time. Would you mind meeting me? At the church, I mean. We could drive to the reception together in your car." The day following her potentially hazardous exploits with the Rapid Transit District, she'd played it smart by picking up a rental car.

She nodded and handed him their plates loaded with luscious cheesecake. "That sounds fine."

Drew carried their plates to the round oak table in the corner of the kitchen.

"How did they meet?" she asked once they were seated.

Drew laughed, the sound open, honest and three times more erotic than any aphrodisiac found on the market. "Maggie was one of Cale's damsels in distress."

"Maggie?" She shook her head, confused. "I thought his fiancée's name was Amanda."

Drew cut into the cheesecake and took a bite. His eyes widened, indicating his pleasure. "She is," he said after a moment. "Maggie is, or *was*, the identity she assumed until her real memory returned about a week or two later."

Emily nibbled on the scrumptious cheesecake while

she listened with rapt attention to Drew as he shared Cale's former penchant for rescuing women. This quirk explained why he hadn't hesitated to offer Amanda a place to live following an accident at a paint warehouse. The incident had caused her temporary memory loss. According to Drew, the memories Amanda did recover were those of the character of her next novel. To Emily's surprise, one of her favorite suspense novelists, Adam Lawrence, was the pseudonym of Cale's fiancée.

"Cale fell hard for her," Drew said, finishing off the last of his cheesecake. A covetous light entered his sexy green eyes as he eyed the large portion still on her own plate. "I think he'd have eventually proposed even if she'd been the hardened criminal she wanted us to believe she was." Instead of sliding her share across the table for him, she sliced into the dessert then held the fork to his lips.

"What about your oldest brother?" she asked him. "Is he married?"

He refused the bite she offered, instead taking the utensil from her fingers and holding the tempting dessert to her lips. Her gaze locked with his. She opened her mouth and slowly leaned forward until the cheesecake teased her tongue. In a blatant, brazen move, she seductively closed her lips around the fork and gently slid the confection onto her tongue, issuing a husky moan of delight, practically guaranteeing the launch of his imagination.

Mission accomplished, she thought with a small satisfied smile. When the color of his eyes brightened as they filled with desire, she threw accelerant on the smoldering embers by using the tip of her tongue to lick away a tiny smudge of the creamy dessert lingering on the edge of the fork.

She had no illusions of a future with Drew, but had decided that stumbling through life in fear of suffering the fallout from another relationship gone south, for whatever reason, was no way to live. Okay, so maybe her handful of previous lovers had had some pretty odd quirks and strange habits a little too distasteful for her liking. That didn't necessarily translate to them being bad guys, they just weren't the right guys for her.

Drew might not be the right guy for her, either. She really wasn't prepared to hazard a guess, but she refused to continue fighting her attraction to him. She didn't believe she was foolish enough to have actually lost all of her common sense and fallen in love, but she did harbor feelings for him that extended beyond basic sexual attraction.

He cleared his throat. "What was your question?" he asked, his voice slightly raspy.

"I asked if your oldest brother was married."

"The only way some woman will ever get Ben to the altar would be to bind and gag him first."

Not exactly the direction she'd wanted their conversation to take, especially when attempting to seduce a man into her bed. "A confirmed bachelor, huh?"

He glanced down at the fork in his hand, then set it on the napkin. His lips tipped upward in a smile so wicked her breath caught.

"Forget my brother." He dipped his finger in the cheesecake. "Forget forks, too."

Drawing air into her lungs took effort, but he'd accepted her challenge and she wasn't about to back down now. Just as she'd done with the fork, she leaned forward and eased her lips over his sensual offering. With aching slowness, she sucked hard on his finger, then slid her tongue around and around the dessert, the sugary confection dissolving in her mouth as she pulled away.

He made a sound that could have been a sigh of pleasure or a hiss of agony. Desire, hot and liquid, simmered inside her, more intense than the late-summer heatwave, and twice as liberating.

"Conversation is overrated," she murmured, a half second before her breathing stalled.

His gaze intent, he stood and slowly circled the table. She rose and met him halfway. With her arms around his neck, she sought his mouth like a heat-seeking missile. He held her hips lightly as he backed her up against the countertop, then gently lifted her onto the cool surface. Impatiently, he nudged her legs apart and stepped between them before urging her bottom to the edge of the counter.

His tongue mated thoroughly with hers as she rocked her hips against the hard ridge of his erection that pressed insistently against the fly of his khaki trousers. Her soft moan sounded more like a strangled cry of need, but she'd zipped past caring the second she'd licked dessert from his finger.

She wanted Drew. Wanted him inside her, wanted

him to fuel the heat between them until they were consumed by the flames. The intensity of the clawing need twisting in her belly had her wet, moist, ready for the ease of his body sliding into hers.

Never had she experienced such a deep, primal desire to mate. She'd mistakenly believed her guard had been up, but somehow, Drew had broken past her imaginary barriers and marked her soul, leaving his imprint on her heart.

His mouth seduced her. The glide of his hands over her body tantalized and teased. With lightning speed, she raced across the line of common sense. The pursuit of pleasure took precedent over lists and goals. The fulfillment of the insistent demands of her body outweighed rational thought by the ton.

She tugged the hem of his navy-blue polo shirt from his trousers, reached beneath the knit fabric and smoothed her hands over his torso while he made her crazy by nipping and laving at her throat, the lobe of her ear, then along her jawline.

The texture of his skin, the muscle beneath her fingertips, the intoxicating, arousing scent of him, lifted her to a new level of awareness. The need to feel her breasts against the solid wall of muscle singlemindedly drove her. In record time, she eased away from him to whip off her T-shirt. She tossed the garment somewhere over his shoulder, not bothering to look despite the rattle of glassware when it landed.

He sucked in a sharp breath as she reached behind her to unfasten her bra. "No," he whispered. "Not yet."

She cried out in a wild combination of mindless pleasure and heated frustration as his mouth trailed a path of burning kisses down her throat to her breasts. Through the pink-floral satin material, he palmed her breast and traced his thumb around her already taut nipple. She arched her back and boldly wrapped her legs around his hips, urging him closer. When he pushed the cup aside and took her into the silky, heated warmth of his mouth, her world tilted. Her senses went haywire, spinning out of control from a determined battle of hedonistic desire and mind-blowing pleasure.

Without an ounce of inhibition, she grasped his hand holding her hip and guided him toward her moist, dewy center to assuage the keen ache building inside her.

With agonizing gentleness, he massaged her inner thigh, easing his hand beneath the restrictive fabric of her denim walking shorts. "More," she whispered in his ear. She rocked her hips forward. "I want more." She wanted her four stars back.

His big hand only reached so far. Enough to tease her mercilessly. Enough to amplify the erotic tug of desire in her belly. She cried out in frustration and reached for the snap of her shorts. As if someone had pumped up the volume, when he unzipped her, the sound of the metal teeth echoed around them.

Somewhere in the back of her mind, where their labored breathing and the rustle of denim as she wiggled out of her shorts pierced her thin thread of consciousness, she marveled at her impatience.

She hooked her now-bared thigh over his hip and brought him close. His mouth caught hers again, capturing her moan of carnal pleasure as his fingers slipped beneath the band of her panties. He teased and coated her feminine folds with her own moisture, alternating the pressure until her body quaked with the need for release.

She tore her mouth from his and clung to his wide shoulder. Her breath came in sharp hard pants as her nerve endings burned and every muscle in her body tightened in anticipation. Just when she believed she'd never survive the excruciating ecstasy for one more second, he eased past her slick folds and slid his fingers deep inside her.

She called his name, crying out from the sheer earth-shattering force of her release. Her hips jerked hard against his hand, over and over as her body clenched tightly around him. He whispered indecipherable words to her, but her muddled senses only managed to heed the gentle, coaxing timbre of his voice and the warmth of his breath against her ear. Wave after wave of sheer bliss tore through her body, rendering the final barriers surrounding her heart to nothing more substantial than kindling, stripping her of any remnants of doubt.

The sweetness with which he eased her back to earth made her heart ache. As her breathing returned to a less life-threatening level, a twinge of embarrassment due to her wild, almost primal response to his incredibly selfless lovemaking, nudged her.

He must have sensed her retreat, because he tucked

his hand beneath her chin and gently urged her head up until she had no choice but to look at him. His tender smile, the gentleness of his gaze, the caring way he righted what was left of her clothing were her undoing. Tears she didn't understand blurred her vision.

"Don't be embarrassed, honey," he said quietly. "You're a beautiful, passionate woman, and that's nothing to be ashamed of."

A chill passed over her exposed skin and she trembled. "I'm not ashamed." Much.

He moved away to retrieve the T-shirt she'd flung halfway across the room, then helped her slip it over her head. She eased off the counter to recover her shorts, wondering how on earth she was supposed to explain the riotous emotions crowding her?

His hand settled on her arm when she attempted to scoot past him. She needed space. Time. Time to regain her composure and locate her common sense. Time to tamp down her stupid heart lodged in her throat.

"Emily? What's going on?"

"This wasn't supposed to happen," she said, knowing she was making a mess of things, but she couldn't think straight when he was so close. It was only supposed to be about sex.

Confusion filled his gaze when she walked to the opposite end of the kitchen. "What specifically wasn't supposed to happen?" he asked.

I wasn't supposed to fall for you. "Let's talk about something else, okay?"

He frowned and moved slowly toward her. "Let's not. Do you regret what just happened?"

She let out a sigh. "Of course not." She couldn't possibly regret something so pure and beautiful. No, her regrets stemmed from her inability to protect herself from world-class heartache.

"Then what's the problem?"

Why did he have to be so relentless? Why couldn't he be as predictable as all the others? Oh no. Not Drew. He just *had* to be different, memorable, sneaking under her skin and stealing her heart when she least expected it. "My emotions are running a little high, that's all."

He braced his feet apart and folded his arms over his massive chest. Just her luck, she'd come up against a determined, immoveable hunk of man. "I'm listening."

He might be listening, and regardless of how incredibly touching his attention was, she'd wager he'd be running to save his hide from a love-struck female in no time flat.

"It really doesn't make any sense." She shook her head, as if the action *would* make sense out of the senseless. "I mean, I've only known you for what? Five or six days?"

She hurried around him, and made a beeline for the table, slinking behind it as if the heavy wood would save her from herself.

"Emily?" he prompted, his impatience thinly veiled. "*What* doesn't make any sense?"

She pulled in a deep breath and let it out slowly. "The way I feel about you right now," she admitted in a rush.

The cocky, self-assured grin of a true scoundrel

curved his devilish mouth. "Yeah?" He circled the table, closing the distance between them. "And how is that?"

The fateful words hovered on her tongue. In the face of his teasing arrogance, her common sense magically appeared, allowing her to keep the words in place.

"Forget it." She smiled up at him. "Your ego doesn't need feeding. It's fat enough."

He laughed and pulled her to him, surrounding her with the musky heat of his body. After tipping her world again with another hot, openmouthed kiss that did nothing to stem the flow of heat already simmering in her veins again, he gazed down at her, the angles of his handsomely chiseled features softened by the tenderness banked in his green eyes. "Nobody ever said it's supposed to make sense."

She swallowed.

Hard.

No way were they on the same page. Really, they couldn't possibly be. Except the gentle, almost possessive way he held her in his arms, told another story entirely. Maybe not one that concluded with happily ever after, but a story that definitely left her with the distinct impression she wasn't the only one delusional, suffering with illusions of having fallen in love.

10

EMILY FASTENED the onyx bracelet she'd borrowed from her grandmother around her wrist, then took one last critical look in the full-length mirror. Funny, she didn't look anywhere near as nervous as her twittering insides indicated.

With the bulk of her wardrobe in New York until she made arrangements to ship her belongings, she'd gone shopping. None of her lightweight casual wear she'd packed for what was supposed to have only been a vacation, would've been appropriate. If the wedding had been a daytime event, one of her ultracomfortable, soft floral skirts might have sufficed, but an after-five affair required a little more elegance.

After breakfast with her grandmother, she'd taken off for Montana Avenue, browsing through the shops and exclusive boutiques, coveting at least a dozen dresses too far out of her budget, until she'd finally unearthed a rich teal, short-sleeved linen sheath at a deep discount. Her budget willpower deserted her like a rat escaping a sinking ship the moment she spied a pair of to-die-for strappy designer heels in black. A little haggling later, she'd managed to talk the store manager down from the original price tag, but she'd blown the savings on an adorable beaded evening bag.

One more spritz of hair spray to ensure the French twist she'd struggled with for almost an hour remained in place, and she declared herself ready. If only her trembling hands agreed. Her case of nerves couldn't completely be attributed to the prospect of meeting Drew's family. Some of the blame lay at his feet. Or rather, at the foot of his bed, because he'd made it perfectly clear she'd be in it once the bouquet had been tossed and the last bottle of champagne had been drained.

She hadn't seen Drew since that night in the kitchen. There were no evening classes for him to teach on Thursday or Friday and for the purpose of maintaining Drew's anonymity, Dave Byrd was handling the investigation, so there had been no excuse to see Drew. She'd been busy Thursday night fussing unnecessarily over her grandmother, and last night he'd spent the time with his brothers and friends at Cale's bachelor party.

He'd surprised her by calling shortly after midnight, and she'd been slightly bemused that he hadn't sounded the least bit tipsy. She'd teased him about the bachelor party, but he maintained the code of the good ol' boys club and hadn't spilled a single detail. Not that she had any right even to question him, but she'd heard enough wild stories from some of the men she used to work with, that she had her suspicions about what really transpired.

She crossed the room to the antique dresser and checked her bag a final time, making sure the little silver foil packets were safely hidden inside the interior zippered pouch. Her midnight call from Drew had entailed a whole lot more than some gentle teasing, and enough verbal foreplay to leave her with no misconceptions about exactly where she'd be spending tonight.

"No regrets," she whispered to her reflection. As she had told Annie that morning when she'd called to update her friend on recent events, a night of mutual gratification did not equate to a broken heart. Just because she and Drew were about to officially become lovers on a grand scale did not mean her heart would end up tangled in the sheets. Not much, anyway.

If she continued to analyze the situation, she'd go nuts. She needed to relax now, or she'd spoil the evening instead of embarking on a journey which included incredible lovemaking with a man who stole her breath.

And your heart.

She ignored her conscience in favor of a deep steadying breath before she yanked open the door to her bedroom, stepped into the hallway and walked confidently into the living room.

Calm.

Serene.

A bundle of nerves.

Grandy rested on the sofa, the cast that ran from her ankle to her knee elevated on a mound of pillows. She listened as Rita discussed the exam she'd given her class the day before. From the way Rita's voice quavered, she was apparently still quite upset by the results. As Emily had discovered yesterday when she'd found Rita near tears after the students had departed, the thirty-something instructor blamed herself for her students failing the class. Margo, quite seasoned after years of working for the Norris Culinary Academy, held no such illusions, and blamed summer blues for the barely passing grades of Rita's students.

"I know it wasn't a final grade, but I'm just not sure what to do." Rita's voice trembled. "I've never had to fail so many students at one time."

"Sounds to me like they weren't paying attention," Margo offered helpfully, then looked up at Emily. "My, don't you look lovely."

Emily smiled, ignoring the curiosity in the elder instructor's pale gaze. "Thank you. I didn't realize you were here."

"We only stopped by for a short visit," Rita said before glancing down at her wristwatch. "And we've overstayed our welcome."

Grandy waved her hand at Rita when she stood. "Sit. I'm enjoying the diversion."

"We really should be going so you can rest." Margo followed Rita to the door. "Think about what we discussed, Velma."

"There's nothing for me to consider." Grandy's voice held a barely perceptible chill that snagged Emily's attention. "I have no interest in retiring."

"Just think about it," Margo pressed. "I would love to help out, so if you change your mind, you know where to find me."

Emily sat in the chair Rita had vacated and waited

until the door closed behind the other women. "What was that all about?" she asked her grandmother.

"Margo suggested I consider taking on a partner."

This was news to Emily, but the idea made sense. "And?"

"I'd rather not have a partner."

Emily nodded and said, "Personally, I think if you wanted a partner, Rita would be more than capable of running the place. At least from what I've seen of her this week." Granted, the woman tended to be a little emotional, but she was competent, organized and she cared about the students.

Grandy let out a sigh. "You're probably right, but..."

"But—" Emily grinned "—the academy is your baby and you're not about to turn it loose, right?"

"Something like that." Grandy laughed. "Now if you were interested..."

"Me?" Now it was Emily's turn to laugh. "Why all the sudden confidence?"

Grandy reached over and pulled a sheaf of papers from the coffee table. "Before Rita and Margo stopped by, I was reading this status report you wrote. After only one week, you've shown me you don't need to cook in order to operate a cooking school effectively."

Emily hadn't done anything special, just together some data from the records and reports she'd reviewed that week and summarized them for her grandmother's review. During regular session, school enrollment hovered close to one hundred students. Recently it had dropped nearly forty percent.

Grandy tapped the page with the tip of her finger.

"This ad you put in the *Times* alone has garnered us eight new student applications for the fall semester, and that's only after two days."

Emily waved away her grandmother's praise. "I *am* in advertising, Grandy. All that means is I have a pretty good idea of how to catch someone's attention. If you could afford radio ads, I suspect you might just double your current enrollment."

"How much?"

Emily shrugged. "I have a few ideas, but let me do some checking first and I'll get back to you. But I'll warn you now, airtime can be fairly expensive. I'd suggest you wait to see what kind of numbers you have for the fall enrollment. If the print ad brings in more students, then I think you could probably justify the expense for the spring semester."

"Let's keep it in mind, then."

She gave her grandmother a look filled with mock sternness. "Maybe Margo isn't too far off base. You should've retired years ago."

Grandy returned Emily's stern expression with one of her own. "I don't teach as much as I used to."

"The administration alone is a full-time job," Emily attempted to reason. Eighty years old was long past the age of retirement, although she greatly admired her grandmother's capabilities. "Maybe you *should* consider at least hiring another instructor or taking on a partner. If not Margo, then talk to Rita."

Grandy folded her arms. "I don't know why everyone is suddenly under the misguided impression I'm getting old and feeble."

Emily laughed despite the seriousness of their conversation. "Older, but never feeble," she said. She stood and crossed the room, crouching in front of her grandmother. "I love you, Grandy. I'd like to see you take some time to enjoy yourself. Take a few vacations. Travel. At least if you had a business partner, you'd have more freedom."

"The only partner I'd consider taking on is you, my dear. And you're not interested, although I really think you should be the one reconsidering."

Emily stood and smoothed her hands down her dress. "I need to be going or I'll be late. Where's Suzette?" she asked, wondering where the caregiver had gone.

"Don't you think this conversation is over yet, young lady."

"Yes, ma'am. Suzette?"

"I sent her to the pier for fried shrimp and chips for our supper tonight," she said with a conspiratorial wink. "She'll be back any minute now. You go. Don't keep that handsome fella waiting."

At that moment, a soft knock at the door announced Suzette's return. Emily opened the door to the tantalizing aroma of deep-fried seafood, her grandmother's favorite naughty treat. "You shouldn't be eating that," she scolded Grandy. "Do you know how much cholesterol there is in it?"

Suzette, a widowed, middle-aged grandmother of nine, rushed through the living room into the kitchen to set their bounty on the oak table. "If anyone at the agency finds out I even agreed to this, I'd lose my job,"

Suzette teased. "Oh God, Velma. You were right. This is going to be fabulous."

"Did you remember the coleslaw?" Grandy called.

Confident her grandmother was in capable, albeit conspiratorial hands, Emily reached into her evening bag for her keys. "You two have fun."

Suzette carried in a lap tray. The china plate nearly overflowed with deep-fried, beer-battered shrimp and French fries.

Emily felt for the zippered enclosure filled with the reminder of the night ahead, then closed the magnetic snap on her bag. "I left Drew's cell number by the phone," she told Suzette. "If you need me, call right away."

"Go." Grandy shooed her away. "Stop fussing, Emily. We'll be fine."

Emily hesitated at the door. Although there hadn't been any incidents all week, she still worried, more so now that Grandy was home. There hadn't been any ground gained in the investigations, either, but at least the cops were still sending extra patrols through the area. "Don't let her talk you out of calling me if she needs anything," she told Suzette. To her grandmother she said, "I'll check in with you later."

"You'll do no such thing," Grandy warned stubbornly. She closed her eyes and moaned in delight as she bit into a fat shrimp.

"Don't worry," Suzette said as she carried her own tray into the living room. "We're not going to do anything more taxing than play a little Scrabble and watch some television."

With nothing left to say, Emily opened the door and walked into the sultry warmth of the late-afternoon sunshine. A light breeze teased the leaves of the mulberry tree, a sure sign the sweltering heatwave had finally begun to ebb.

She reached the rental car and smiled to herself, wondering what her grandmother would think of the three condoms tucked inside her purse, then laughed as she slid into the driver's seat. She'd probably scold her...because she hadn't brought the entire box.

DREW HAD KNOWN Cale and Amanda's wedding would rival a circus, but couldn't help but admire his new sister-in-law's attention to detail in putting it all together, and on such a grand scale, in only three months. Her father, Lawrence Hayes, had spared no expense for his only daughter's wedding. As many as four hundred guests celebrated the marriage of Cale and Amanda with the finest cuisine prepared by the city's top chefs. Champagne, rumored to be nothing less than Dom Perignon, which Drew hadn't touched, flowed freely from an elaborate crystal fountain. The guests were as varied as the music, ranging from the crème de la crème of New York society to blue-collar Americana.

"Are you having a good time?" Drew whispered against Emily's ear as they swayed with the rhythm of an old love song.

"Hmm," she murmured. "The best. But my feet are starting to protest."

He eased away from her to cast a quick glance down at her feet, which looked to be a tad swollen.

"New shoes," she explained.

"Why don't we sit this one out and get some air?"

With his hand on her back, he steered her from the crowded dance floor as the music changed to a more lively, upbeat tempo.

"Now this," she said, "is the best proposition I've had in a while."

He stopped and looked down at her. "You've had others?" he asked carefully. Surely that wasn't jealousy creeping up his back and making his neck tense?

Her smile widened and she laughed. "Hardly," she said loud enough to be heard over the din of the music. "I was referring to my brush last weekend with the world's oldest profession."

The sharp gasp from a pair of blue-haired ladies at a nearby table, followed by narrow eyed stares sent her into a fit of the giggles.

Drew relaxed.

"I hope you weren't related to them," she said. Once they cleared the ballroom, she stopped to slip off her shoes. He didn't bother to tell her she'd never get them back on her feet considering the rate they were swelling. "Otherwise the good impression I made on your aunt was for nothing."

"You're safe," he told her, taking her hand. "I've never seen them before." And probably never would again, nor three-quarters of the other guests in attendance.

The night air was warm, tangy from the sea and

filled with the heavy perfume of roses. They walked quietly along a flagstone path and wandered through the hotel's famed rose garden until they reached the stone-and-wrought-iron gazebo. Emily sat on one of the lower steps and patted the space next to her. Instead, he sat behind her and urged her to rest her back against him.

He leaned forward and whispered in her ear. "Have I told you how beautiful you are?"

She tipped her head back to look up at him, a sweet smile on the lips he'd been anxious to taste all night.

"Sure you have." A teasing light entered her eyes. "Every single time I ask you about the bachelor party."

Drew chuckled. "It's called changing the subject."

Her eyebrows hiked upward. "More like avoiding the subject. So, were there naked women?"

No way would he tell her there were plenty of them—in varying degrees of undress—but they'd all remained on the stage. A definite look-but-no-touching-allowed situation. Bachelor parties at Lula's were a tradition for the guys at Trinity Station. They might get a little loud, but their behavior never extended beyond a few raunchy comments.

He gave her a sly grin. "My aunt adores you," he said, *changing* the subject. He'd been required to sit at the table with the wedding party, so he'd left Emily in his aunt's care. The moment he'd been free of his obligations as a groomsman, Debbie hadn't hesitated to let him know she'd enjoyed Emily's company. He hadn't realized he'd been seeking her approval, but her words still left him with a sense of contentment he hadn't expected.

"She's very sweet," Emily said as she snuggled closer. "She couldn't stop talking about you. Tilly wasn't too happy with her, though." She grinned. "Debbie told me about some of the scrapes the two of you got into when you were kids. You guys were awful."

He and Tilly had been known as the neighborhood terrors. "We couldn't have been all that bad, since we only had the cops called on us once."

"Isn't that enough?" Emily's lyrical laughter carried on the sea breeze, floating around him, drawing him deeper under her bewitching spell. "Burying the neighbor's garden gnomes in her yard—complete with headstones—*and* rearranging her rose bushes? Really, Drew. That's some prank."

"The roses were Tilly's idea. And we did it to avenge Cale because the old bat reported him to animal control for having too many pets," he offered in their defense. "Tilly and her dad lived next door so she spent a lot of time at our house. It was kind of like having a sister."

He quieted as the sound of footsteps neared. Drew glanced up in time to see Ben heading down the path toward them, an amber bottle clutched in his hand, his bow tie hanging loose around his collar. He acknowledged them with a brief wave, then turned down the path toward the marina.

"Is he okay?" Emily asked, keeping her voice low,

just loud enough for Drew to hear. "I noticed he didn't bring a date."

He shook his head. "He hasn't dated in a while."

"Some woman do a number on him?"

More like Ben doing some number on a woman. His oldest brother had been in a serious relationship or two, but the second he caught a whiff of the marriage vibe, he booked. "No," he said. "My old man."

He didn't need to look down into Emily's face to see the confusion knitting her brow. He could feel it in the way she tipped her head back and waited for him to continue.

Maybe for comfort, maybe because he simply wanted her soft skin against his, he smoothed his hands down her arms to her hands and laced their fingers together. "When my mom died, my dad gave up—on everything," he admitted. "I was too young to really understand much about what was going on at the time, but Ben was older and he weathered a lot more than Cale and I ever did."

She turned forward again and settled her back against his chest. "You mentioned your mother was a firefighter."

"She was one of the first in the county, back at the beginning of the women's movement. My aunt told me once the county tried to railroad Mom into an admin job, but Mom fought. After some hotshot women's rights attorney came forward and threatened a discrimination suit, the county backed off and Mom became a full-fledged firefighter."

"You should be proud of her. She was a real pioneer for women's rights."

"Absolutely," he said, and meant it. "But all I knew then was that Mom had the same job as Dad."

She traced her thumb over his in a soothing, rhythmic motion. "Do you remember her?"

"Some things. The way she smelled mostly. Like fresh laundry and lilacs. Most of what I know, though, I've been told. I do remember being at the hospital." He suppressed a shudder as the darkest memories swamped him. "I still can't stand being there for any length of time."

"I didn't know," she whispered, urging his arms tighter around her. "You stayed the entire time I was there with Grandy. You should've said something."

His mild laughter held only a hint of humor. "And admit to you my armor's tarnished? Not a chance, babe."

"I can't even begin to image what you and your brothers must've gone through."

"It was rough on everyone. Mom hung on for three days," he said, "which is saying a lot for someone with such extensive third-degree burns. All the doctors could do was try to make her as comfortable as possible."

"I'm so sorry."

The compassion in her voice warmed him, urging him to continue to sift through the memories. "My mom was on the first team at the scene of a big fire in the garment district. By the time the crew arrived, the fire had already started to spread to a neighboring warehouse, which was supposedly vacant. My folks worked for different stations, but this was a monster burn so they called in engine crews from all over the county to assist. My dad's was one of them.

"Some homeless people had been living in the abandoned warehouse and were trapped on one of the upper floors. Mom, Dad and two other firefighters went in on the first rescue team. She saved the transients, but before she could get out, either the floor or the roof collapsed and she was trapped. Dad tried to get to her, but her helmet had been knocked off."

He pulled in a deep breath and held Emily close, next to his heart, a place he realized had been empty for far too many years. "The smoke inhalation was bad, and her burns were too extensive."

"They didn't let you see her, did they?"

He shook his head, then realized she couldn't see him. "No," he said. "She wouldn't let us. I didn't understand then, but I guess she said she didn't want her sons' last memory of her to be something out of a nightmare. But she did try to talk to us on the phone, though. My aunt held the phone for her, and Mom managed to say a few words to all three of us. Mostly goodbye. She died later that night."

Emily trembled in his arms. He knew the feeling. Gooseflesh still prickled his skin whenever he thought of that night and the horrible days that followed.

"The old man never got over it." The sharp edge of resentment still managed to nudge him, making his voice harder than he'd intended. "I remember he did try for a while, for our sakes, I suppose, but even we figured out pretty quickly he was only going through the motions. About two years after we lost Mom, he died of a massive coronary. At least that's what the death certificate says."

"What do you mean?"

"The day of Mom's funeral was the last time my dad ever wore his uniform. He climbed inside a bottle of gin and never came out again. Ben took care of us. He bullied us into doing our homework and taking our baths, made sure we had clean clothes to wear to school and enough to eat. And when he wasn't looking after us, he was holding my old man's head over the toilet while he puked his brains out, or fending off creditors because my dad couldn't be bothered to take care of it himself. I found out years later that Ben started forging my dad's name on checks just to keep the bills paid every month."

"My God, Drew," she gasped. "How old was he?"

"Ten. Twelve when we went to live with Debbie. You know, you'd have thought he'd be relieved to have her taking care of us, but Ben refused to let go. I think he'd shouldered the responsibility for so long, he didn't know how to stop. He made Debbie's life hell for a while. It took him a long time to trust her enough to let her take care of us."

He smiled suddenly, struck by an odd sense of relief. All she'd done was listen, but Emily accomplished what a bevy of high-priced child psychologists hadn't—allowed him to exorcize demons he'd carted around for far too long. "Ben still hasn't stopped trying to tell us what to do. He really needs to get a life and stay out of mine and Cale's."

"Maybe he'll get lucky," she said after a gentle sigh. "He could find the right woman someday."

Drew had his doubts, but he wasn't going to dash Emily's romantic hopes for his big brother. "We've wasted enough moonlight talking about Ben." He liked the way she'd styled her hair and took advantage of all that exposed skin by dipping his head to nuzzle her nape, his intent to turn her into a puddle of need.

Her breath caught, and she tilted her head slightly to the side. With her back still to him, she eased her hands from his and lifted them over her head to loop around his neck. She arched her back, thrusting her breasts forward in an inviting display he didn't even attempt to resist.

"There you two are!"

The abrupt intrusion of Tilly's cheery voice split them apart faster than a pair of guilty teenagers caught necking in the back seat of a Chevy. "What do you want?" he groused. Not that Tilly would take offense. The concept had never existed between the two of them.

"We were sent to scout the missing-in-action," Scorch offered sheepishly as he and Tilly neared the gazebo. "Amanda's gonna show some leg."

Apparently, they'd kissed and made up.

Emily winced as she attempted, unsuccessfully, to slide her feet into her shoes. "You go ahead," she said. "I'll never get my feet back into their torture chambers."

"Ouch," Tilly said sympathetically. "Just forget the shoes, Em." She stepped forward and took hold of Emily's hand, pulling her to her feet. "Your presence has been commanded, so you'll just have to go in your stockings. And it's not about Amanda showing some leg," she scolded Scorch. "It's about bouquets and garters."

Drew grinned. Not that he was looking to snag the garter for himself, but the traditional bouquet and garter toss signified the bride and groom would soon retire to the honeymoon suite—and he would finally have Emily to himself.

11

IF EMILY continued to wiggle her backside against him, Drew had no doubts his control would become a thing of the past. "You have to hold still, sweetheart."

"This is *so* not comfortable," she complained. She moved again. "I think you've got too much."

He readjusted the ice pack he held to her temple. "Just a little longer." He chuckled when she eased out an impatient huff of breath. "If you'd been paying attention, this wouldn't have happened."

She snatched the ice pack from his hand, tossed it in the sink, then gingerly inspected the small lump with her fingertips. "How was I supposed to know your sister-in-law had an arm to rival a major-league pitcher?"

Tilly had actually caught the wedding bouquet, horrifying his buddy, Scorch. Emily only managed to get herself whacked in the head by the hard plastic holder when it came flying like a fastball in her and Tilly's direction. Drew didn't know which of the two women Amanda had been aiming for, and he wasn't sure he wanted to, either. Tradition dictated the woman who caught the bride's bouquet would be the next to marry. If there was any truth to the silly custom, he pitied the pressure Scorch would face, but breathed his own sigh of relief that Emily hadn't been paying attention.

He handed her a glass half filled with 7Up. "Will you live?"

"Oh, I think so." She took a sip of the soft drink, then smiled. "Hey, maybe I can use the lethal-bouquet incident in a pain reliever ad someday."

He took her hand and led the way out of the kitchen to the living room. Once seated on the supple black Italian-leather sofa, he tapped the remote control to start the light jazz CD in the stereo system. The dim light of the table lamp cast an unobtrusive, buttery glow, enhancing the sultry ambiance.

Emily curled up beside him on the sofa. He could get used to this, he thought, wondering how it would feel to come home at the end of the day into the waiting arms of one special woman.

He scoffed at the idea. Weddings made people sappy, did strange things to their psyches. Just because Cale had become a proponent of matrimony didn't mean he was destined to follow in his footsteps. Did it?

"So who're your decorators?" she asked, tucking her feet beneath her, then resting her head against his shoulder. "Spartan, Bare and Sterile?"

He held her close, breathing in her scent as he looked around the room. "That bad, huh?"

"That bad."

Compared to her grandmother's place, which had a welcoming lived-in feel, he supposed his condo did come across as somewhat impersonal. The living room, dining area and kitchen were open, with high pickled-oak-slat ceilings. A bank of east windows allowed for plenty of light and offered a nightly panoramic view of the city below.

"It's easy," he said. "What's not to like?" He'd never cared one way or another what anyone thought of his condo, but Emily's opinion suddenly mattered—a lot.

"It's a nice place," she said. "If it were me, though, I'd definitely add a few splashes of color. Maybe not get rid of all the black leather furniture, but definitely ditch these wrought-iron-and-glass tables. You could spruce it up some with a few personal touches so it looks like someone actually lives here."

Maybe she had a point, he thought. Unlike Cale and Ben, both of whom displayed family photos in their homes, above his black-and-gray-marble mantel hung a Jackson Pollock abstract print. Cale and Amanda's living room was often cluttered with books, and of late, bridal magazines and travel brochures. He suspected in the near future parenting magazines and children's coloring books would be added to the fray. Nothing marred the clear surface of his glass cocktail table.

Plain black wrought-iron pole lamps with simple white shades were centered on the matching end tables. Against his will, his imagination conjured Emily removing a handful of toy cars and a forgotten half-eaten cookie from the surfaces. In the dining room, beneath the circular black track lighting, only chairs and the glass-topped table sat, its surface as unremarkable as the cocktail table. In his mind, she placed a ceramic footed bowl filled with fruit in anticipation of a child's small hands in search of a snack.

The sterility of his home had never bothered him.

The clean, simplistic lines and lack of chaos and clutter appealed to him. Didn't it?

Yes, it did, he reminded himself.

Firmly.

Uselessly, too, since he couldn't shake the images of Emily turning his black-and-white existence into a home filled with laughter, splashes of color and loads of chaos.

She reached behind her to set her glass on the tall sofa table, then took his and put it next to hers. "I don't want to talk decorating." She rose to her knees, hiked up her dress so she could straddle his hips, then settled her bottom on his thighs. "In fact," she murmured, "I don't want to talk at all."

A sassy twinkle brightened her gaze, quickening his pulse. Her lips lifted in a wicked, seductive smile filled with an intent he wouldn't dream of resisting. Twice he'd put an end to their lovemaking. Tonight there'd be no stopping them.

"What exactly did you have in mind?" he asked her, but he'd have to be a corpse not to understand her meaning. He'd been wanting, needing the exact same thing from her since the day they'd met on her grandmother's porch.

"Pleasure." One by one, she flicked open the buttons of his shirt, then shoved the fabric aside. She smoothed her hands over the surface of his skin, exploring his torso. Warmth filled his body, traveling in a southerly direction.

"Pleasure is good."

The intriguing cant of her mouth widened as her

hands followed the trail of heat. She cupped her hand over the erection already straining against the confines of his tuxedo trousers. "Passion."

His vocal chords froze, rendering him incapable of speech.

She leaned into him, kissing his neck. Her tongue traced his jaw. "Hot..."

Her fingers explored his length through his trousers, driving him to the brink of insanity.

"Wet..."

There was no mistaking her intention when she rocked her bottom against his thighs. A tiny tremor shook her body at the erotic friction, making him impossibly harder.

"Deep," she whispered. "Very, very deep."

He couldn't breathe.

Her warm breath fanned his skin. "Sex."

He never had a chance to reply, because her mouth caught his, her tongue delving deep inside in fierce sensual demand. Her hands stroked his body, feeding his need. He cupped the back of her head in his hand, slanted his mouth and answered her demand, then demanded more.

He growled in protest when her hands left his body to fumble with something behind him on the sofa table. She whimpered in response, then scooted closer, rocking her hips against him in sexy simulation guaranteed to make him forget everything but the woman pulling him dangerously close to the edge.

The distinct tear of a foil packet rent the electrically charged air around them. By the time she ended the kiss to free him from the confines of his trousers and shorts, he was breathing hard. He stared mesmerized as she held his length in her hand, her fingers wrapped around his shaft. When she sheathed him, he nearly came out of his skin.

This wasn't how he envisioned fully making love to her the first time. He'd planned soft music, softer lights and the smooth luxury of red Egyptian-cotton sheets tangled around their bodies. He'd fantasized over and over having her beneath him, making her his in the most elemental way and watching her eyes as passion shook her. He gladly shoved his fantasies aside for the reality of her holding him in her slender, delicate hands.

The need to touch her intimately too strong to ignore, he slid his hand along the inside of her thigh, kneading the soft flesh as he inched closer to her moist heat.

A hiss of breath left his lungs in a rush. No satin or lace impeded his progress when his fingers found her dewy center. "Damn." The single word came out a strained whisper. "No panties?"

Slowly, she moved her head from side to side. "Panty hose." A soft moan interrupted her explanation when he separated her folds to slick his thumb over her most sensitive place. "Ruined," she rasped. "Totally trashed."

Whether it was the image of Emily wearing no panties beneath her elegant dress that stole his breath, or the way she closed her eyes, tossed her head back and strained toward his exploring fingers, he couldn't say, but he highly suspected both had a great deal to do with the throbbing of his erection. About all he could manage himself was a growl of appreciation for the sensual woman making him crazy with desire.

With her hands on his shoulders, she rose up on her knees again, granting him deeper access. Her body was hot, slick, growing wetter with each stroke of his fingers, each slide of his thumb over her folds.

"Come with me this time." Her voice had grown huskier, more strained and sexier than even he'd imagined in his fantasies. He applied pressure to her swollen center. The pitch of her gentle moan of pleasure rose a full octave. He knew from their previous encounter, Emily could never be classified as a quiet lover, but never had the sound of pleasure filled him with such pure male satisfaction.

Need clawed his gut with greedy fingers. He struggled to hold it at bay for a while longer. Her movements became more demanding, but he held her back, too, prolonging the exquisite tension building inside them.

"I want you inside me," she demanded. "I want to feel you there when I come."

"You will, baby," he promised. "You will." But not yet.

Carefully, he took hold of her hips and eased her away from him. Her eyes filled with protest, until he moved in front of her on the floor and gently scooted her bottom to the edge of the leather.

Her folds glistened with moisture, her body primed for his. He'd never been so uncomfortably hard as he was at this moment with Emily. He eased her thighs open and parted her, exposing the core of her pleasure. He circled and teased her with the tip of his finger, then slid it deep inside her, only to retreat and start again, until her back arched off the sofa.

He changed the pressure, holding her release just far enough out of her reach. Her musky scent rose around him, intoxicating him. He kissed her trembling thigh, then eased her open thighs farther apart before he dipped his head and stroked her heat with his tongue.

She whimpered, but the erotic sound soon coalesced into a primitive moan of deep gratification. He laved and suckled, teased and taunted her as her moisture spilled onto his tongue and the rate of her breathing increased with each deep stroke.

There was nothing gentle in the way she reached for him and pulled him to her, or in the way she took control of their lovemaking. With the skirt of her dress still gathered around her hips, she urged him back onto the sofa, then straddled his hips. She held his erection in her hand and lowered her body, consuming him deep into her slick heat.

Her breath caught and her eyes widened as she accepted the full, long hardness of him. Cupping the silky flesh of her bottom in his hands, he let her set the pace. Her movements were hard and demanding as she rode him, taking him deeper inside. Her soft cries of pleasure built and grew louder from her moist, parted lips, straining his already battered control.

He kept his gaze locked with hers, marveling at the shameless wonder combined with flaming passion with each measured stroke of her body on his. Just when his control slipped to its lowest level, her fingertips dug into his shoulders and she upped the tempo, pushing them both closer to the final pinnacle, closer to the ultimate bliss of release.

The only sound more beautiful than her deep, heavy breathing or her tiny passionate mewls as the tension climbed higher and higher, was the unabashed outcry of pure ecstasy pouring from her mouth and spilling over him when he moved his hands to her hips and held her tight, then thrust upward. He rose to meet her, thrust for thrust, again and again until the fiery orgasm inflamed her completely. She strained, pushing harder against him. She tossed her head from side to side as the molten heat climbed and flowed around him. Her hair tumbled free, falling in a soft, golden cloud past her shoulders, but it was her cries and the tight clenching of her sex milking him that filled his mind seconds before his world exploded, shattering the final thread of his control.

Every cell in his body came vibrantly alive. The heavy beat of his heart pounded in his ears, through his veins. Electrically charged heat pulsed through his body, sending him over the edge with a force he hadn't expected.

Somewhere in the back of his mind, he felt Emily collapse against his chest. He centered on her breathing, as ragged as his own, as he held her close, marveling at the way their bodies remained intimately locked, slowly relaxing from the aftershocks of their loving.

The brush of her lips against his throat was as soft as

the barely decipherable words she whispered against his sweat-moistened skin.

But heaven help him, he'd heard her.

The words penetrated his brain like a death knell, chilling him to the bone, evaporating the warm glow of spent passion. Three little words, the ones he feared hearing the most... "I love you."

DREW STOOD with his hands braced on the pristine white ceramic tile of the kitchen counter, impatiently drumming his fingers, waiting for the coffeemaker to finish its cycle. Emily hadn't stirred in the time it took him to shower and dress. Quite frankly, he was in no mood to awaken her because then he'd have to face her.

He should've sent her packing last night after hearing her gently whispered declaration of love, but he'd compounded his own stupidity by pretending he hadn't heard her. Instead, he'd carried her off to his bed and made love to her until the first gray fingers of dawn touched the darkened sky.

He muttered a vile string of curses capable of shaming even Gilda, the foul-mouthed parrot Cale had rescued. Drew didn't care, not with his red-lining emotions making him edgy. What the hell was he supposed to do now? He hadn't blanched much when he suspected he was falling for her, but to hear her say she loved him... No, he wouldn't accept it. He couldn't, not when he'd sworn a long time ago he could never accept the responsibility of being loved, of being the cause of such deep pain that living became unbearable.

"Good morning."

The sleep-husky sound of Emily's sweet voice startled him, then filled him with more dread. He knew he'd end up hurting her, but consoled himself with the belief that a little hurt now was better than a whole lot of pain later.

With his hands still braced on the counter, he turned his head in her direction. She looked rumpled and way too sensual for his peace of mind. A sexy smile curved her lips, still swollen from his kisses. He recalled some of the most intimate things she'd done with those lips and his lower body flexed with recognition.

Sunshine from the east windows poured into the kitchen, rendering the white button-down shirt she'd liberated from his closet a useless shield to cover her lush curves. The sight of her body outlined beneath the cotton was way too tempting, so he averted his gaze. Unfortunately, his body hardened in a flash from the imprint on his mind, resurrecting memories of the night. Irritation fed his sour mood, probably fueled by his frustrated desire to take advantage of the sight of her long, shapely legs beneath the tail of his shirt.

He straightened and pulled a big black mug from the cabinet. "You should get home. Your grandmother's probably worried." He hadn't meant for the words to come out quite so brusquely, but he couldn't seem to help himself. In the long run, it was better this way. Cut their losses now and move on instead of encouraging emotions he could never accept.

Instead of serving himself a cup of the steaming brew, he foolishly glanced at her in time to see her shock at his harsh words fade into hurt, piercing his heart with all the subtlety of a sledgehammer.

"Drew?" The caution in her voice finished off what little the sledgehammer left behind. "What's going on?"

He poured himself some coffee. "I need to be at my aunt's soon for brunch. Cale and Amanda are opening their wedding gifts, then leaving for their honeymoon. I promised I'd be there." Actually, he'd promised he *and* Emily would be there.

Not going to happen.

She crossed her arms, hiking his shirt up to reveal more of her luscious legs. "As a liar, you suck."

"Come again?" He sipped his coffee, in case his first stall tactic failed. What was so hard about telling the first woman he'd ever really let his guard down enough to actually care about that they wouldn't be seeing each other again? No reason at all he should be avoiding telling her he was about to stomp all over her heart.

His imaginary white charger returned, only to buck him off—in less than eight seconds.

"You're not a very good liar." She lowered her arms and tilted her hip to the side before resting her hand on the counter. Her gaze filled with suspicion. "I don't think you rushing me out of here has anything to do with my grandmother worrying about me or brunch with your family."

Okay, so he possessed all the subtly of a sledgehammer, as well. He let out a weighty sigh and set his mug on the counter. The morning had started out bad and was about to get worse, but there wasn't a damned thing he could do to change it.

"Look, Emily—"

"No," she interrupted him hotly, her eyes filling with fire and suspicion. "You look. Everything was fine between us last night. What? Did you finally remember that I told you I loved you? Is that why you're pulling away from me so fast I'm choking on the vapor trail?"

The shrill ring of the phone stilled the denial—or the truth—on his tongue. He considered answering, if only to give himself more time to summon the right words, but skirting the issue wouldn't benefit either of them. Better to get the deed done and move on with their lives.

Alone.

The ringing stopped, and she glanced down at the red digital display. The indicator showed seven waiting messages. When she looked his way again, her distaste mocked him. The anger simmering in her gaze left his conscience scorched.

"You're so terrified of some woman putting a noose around your neck, I bet all those waiting messages are from poor unsuspecting fools suffering with rope burn."

"You're wrong," he argued, but the staunch ring of truth in her statement took the heat out of his words. She'd nailed it, hard. He'd studiously avoided anything that remotely resembled a serious relationship for years.

In an angry gesture, she shoved a wavy lock of her

blond hair from her face. "Is that why you're giving me the cold shoulder? You're afraid I've got a noose hidden in my purse? Because unless I'm really reading you all wrong, I know you care about me, too."

"It's not..." *that I don't care about you.* The words froze in his throat, then spread with icy fingers to circle his heart. It wasn't that he didn't care about her, because he did. A great deal. If he didn't, then they wouldn't be having this conversation.

"Did I ask you to burn your little black book?" She pushed off the counter and advanced on him until they were red-painted toenails to casual sneakers. "Did I ever once *hint* that I'm looking for marriage or forever?"

If he wasn't fighting for his survival, and hers, he just might have enjoyed all her spit and fire. "No," he admitted.

"Then *what*—" she emphasized the word by nearly drilling a hole in his chest with her index finger "—is going on inside that head of yours?"

He let out another sigh, and said the words he knew would drive her away. "I don't want your love, Emily."

12

EMILY COULDN'T have been more stunned if Drew had slapped her. At least emotionally. A hard sucker punch right to her heart, because she'd swear it had physically shattered into a trillion fragments at his softly spoken words.

I don't want your love, Emily.

She backed away from him, her leaden feet moving slowly until her backside came in contact with the cabinets behind her. Those awful words reverberated through her soul. The distance did nothing to create the blessed numbness she craved to protect what was left of her heart, or to ease the chill creeping over her flesh. How could she have been so wrong—again?

"Then there's nothing left for me to say." Much to her surprise, her voice didn't tremble. She couldn't say the same for her limbs. "I'll just get my things."

She walked away, but she really wanted to sit down and weep. The need to get as far away from Drew, to put as much distance as humanly possible from the pain of his rejection kept her moving. Escaping the deep ache in her chest wouldn't be quite so simple.

She made it as far as the living room before his voice stopped her. "Emily, wait."

"Don't say anything else. Please." She wouldn't look

at him. To do so would only remind her of how stupid she'd been to think for a minute he'd been different. "My ego has had enough bruises lately."

"I'm sorry."

The words failed to placate, angering her instead. She laughed, but the sound was as cold as the deep freeze already settling around her. "Yeah, me, too."

Before she did something really dumb, like cry in front of him, she took off for the bedroom. By the time she hit the door, her entire body trembled. She was a powder keg of hurt and indignation, embarrassment and frustration, ready to blow at the first strike.

Her hands shook so hard, she had trouble with the buttons of his shirt. With a frustrated hiss, she gave up, pulled the shirt over her head and threw it on the bed. The rumpled, tangled sheets mocked her.

"Dammit," she muttered to herself. Once again, she'd made the wrong choice. With her history, she shouldn't be surprised or even upset. Except this time was different. This time the ramifications would be long-lasting. Unlike her previous relationships, *this time*, she'd actually fallen in love.

After plucking her bra from the floor near the dresser, she padded naked to the other side of the room for her dress, stepping over Drew's clothes along the way. Clothes she'd practically torn from his body. She might not be able to close her eyes and imagine her life without him, but what choice did she have?

He'd made his choice perfectly clear. He didn't want her love.

He didn't want *her*.

Whether more angry with him or herself, she wasn't certain, but she aimed her ire at them both. Her, for being foolish enough to fall in love. Him, for leaving the imprint of his Nikes on her backside as he booted her out the door.

She stepped into her dress and hauled it past her hips before she sat on the edge of the bed to fasten her bra.

"Emily?"

The black lace demi bra dangled from her fingertips. With her dress still hanging loose around her waist, she glanced up as he walked into the room. She should have found at least a modicum of comfort in seeing the misery etched on his handsome face, only she couldn't. Instead, the ache in her chest intensified, making her angry enough to want to throw something at him, preferably a sharp object. Several sharp objects.

He stuffed his hands into the front pockets of his navy trousers. "I know what you're thinking."

Why couldn't he just leave her be? He'd made his position crystal clear. He didn't want her. Fine. She got the message.

She hooked her bra, then set the half cups in place. "Oh?" She yanked the straps over her shoulders. "And what am I thinking?"

"That I'm an inconsiderate ass."

She wasn't about to argue with him. "Add a few more choice words to that description, and you just might be the first man in history to be right about something."

He winced at her sharp words.

"I'm not exactly in the mood for a relationship post-mortem right now." She'd reserve that privilege for later, like when she was alone with a box of tissues and a truckload of self-pity for company.

She stood and shoved her arms into the sleeves of her dress. If she didn't get away from him—and fast, she might just give in to the fantasy of doing him bodily harm.

The deep frown creasing his brow indicated his lack of appreciation for her sarcasm. "I do care about you." He let out a harsh breath, then shoved his hand roughly through his thick, rich hair. "Hell, I might even be in love with you. I don't know. I've never loved someone who wasn't a member of my family."

"Oh, lucky me. I fall in love with a guy who says he loves me, but doesn't want my love. Jeez, Drew. You're making more and more sense by the second." She zipped up her dress, then looked around the room for her shoes. Wasn't there a rule somewhere that stated hurt wasn't supposed to accompany a declaration of love? Apparently the rule book required an addendum.

"You're not helping matters," he complained.

Aha. The toe of one shoe peeked out from beneath the bed. From *his* side of the bed. "Help isn't exactly what I'm aiming for here." She dropped to her knees to ferret out its mate, tossing aside the sheet dangling over the side, only to be overwhelmed by the musky scent of their lovemaking.

"Would you stop for a minute and let me explain?"

She snagged her shoes and stood so fast to escape the

memories of their glorious, passionate night together, the room spun momentarily. "I don't think so," she said, then promptly walked out of the bedroom.

The memories, and Drew, followed.

She found her hairpins scattered over the sofa and floor, then scooped her evening bag from the sofa table to tuck the pins inside the now condomless interior compartment. His big hand settled on her shoulder, urging her to turn around. She did, but refused to look at him. If she did, she feared she'd start sobbing and wouldn't be able to stop.

"Look at me, Emily."

Don't do it. Don't you dare look into those incredible green eyes.

He tucked his finger beneath her chin and gently eased her head upward. Against her will, she stared anyway, stunned into temporary silence by the pain in his eyes, the ache banked there mirroring her own. How could he do this to them? How could he hurt them both this way?

"My dad loved my mom." His velvety-smooth voice, tinged with emotion, diffused her anger—a little. Very little.

"She was everything to him," he continued, lowering his hands to his side. "When she died, so did he. Not physically right away, but he died inside. I might not be the guy on the scene fighting the fires any longer, but there's still an element of danger to my job, Emily. I enter buildings to determine the cause of a burn. There are OSHA restrictions and certain steps taken to ensure my safety, but accidents can still happen.''

She didn't understand. ''What does that have to do with how we feel about each other?''

''What if something happened? What if we did move in together, or married and started a family? What about the baby you're carrying? I'm not going to do to you and your kid what my mom's death did to my family.''

Her jaw dropped. Literally. Her purse and strappy heels slipped from her fingers, clattering to the floor in a series of dull thuds, underscoring her stunned disbelief.

He couldn't possibly be serious.

Could he?

Rubbing her temples with the tips of her fingers did nothing to lessen her confusion. Slowly, she sat down on the edge of the sofa, shaking her head, positively flabbergasted by his revelation.

''Let me get this straight,'' she said when she recovered enough from her shock to speak again. ''You don't want me to love *you* because you think *I'd* fall apart if something happened to you?''

His body visibly tensed. ''Something like that.''

He was putting her through the emotional wringer for that? ''That has to be the most twisted logic in support of commitment atheism I've ever heard.''

''I lived through it, remember?'' His voice rose. Obviously, she'd offended him. ''I've seen for myself what happens because you love someone too much.''

''What you lived through was miserable, yes. You

lost your mother, then witnessed the deterioration of your father. A childhood like that would leave scars on anyone. I get it. But, Drew, did you ever stop to think that some people are emotionally stronger than others?"

He turned his back on her and walked across the room to stand before the empty fireplace. With his hands tucked in his pockets again, his shoulders slumped forward.

"Death is a part of life, and you go on," she told him. She stood and moved toward him, wondering if she had the power to change twenty-some-odd years of a belief system she barely understood. "Yes, we mourn the loss of a loved one, but what your father did was wallow in his own self-pity. Instead of honoring your mother's memory, he destroyed it."

He glanced down when she reached his side. Coldness emanated from him in icy waves. She resisted the urge to shiver.

"You don't know what you're talking about." He spoke quietly, deliberately. "You weren't there."

"No, I wasn't, but you said it yourself—he gave up. And what's worse, he gave up on his sons when they needed him the most. When *you* needed him the most."

"That's right," he shot at her suddenly. "I'll be damned if I'm going to go through...going to cause someone that kind of suffering because they loved me."

His slip couldn't have been any more Freudian, or revealing. Like a surge of electricity, realization jolted her understanding of his reasoning for giving her the boot.

"Oh, you are so full of it!" She ignored his ferocious frown. She had to, she was fighting for her life, her life with him. "What has you running scared is that you're afraid you'll end up just like him. Even though you think you might be in love with me, it's still easier for you to let me walk away than to admit the truth. There's no risk involved that way, is there?"

A flash of panic passed through his eyes before the stone-cold hardness returned, shoving aside the brief glimpse of vulnerability. "That's bull."

"Oh really?" she argued. "You are terrified you'll self-destruct, just like your dad did, and it's crippling you. Well, I have news for you, Drew. If you don't smarten up, you're going to end up a very lonely old man."

"I think you'd better leave now."

The icy threat in his voice sent a warning signal to her brain that she'd pushed him too far, poking and prodding at a still-tender open wound. Well, tough, she thought childishly. She really didn't give a damn. Not because she wanted to hurt him, but unless she managed somehow to evaporate the mist clouding his judgment, he'd never see reality.

The thunderous expression on his face should have had her scooting out the door. Instead, she planted her hands on her hips and returned his glare with one of her own. "Why? So you don't have to face the truth? Or so you don't have to see what you're throwing away because of one man's unhealthy, selfish destruction?"

He uttered a ripe curse, then reached for his beeper vibrating at his side. He muttered more curses before walking away from her. While he picked up the phone and punched numbers into the keypad, she slipped into her shoes and picked up her bag. Unless Drew came to his senses, there really wasn't anything she could do except leave.

"I'm on my way," he said, then hung up the phone.

Nothing subtle about *that*, she thought. Lucky him, he'd been saved from being forced into further introspection. Unlucky her, she'd be nursing a broken heart for the next...oh, fifty, sixty years.

He came back into the living room. "I'm not sure I know how to say this."

"Goodbye." She let out a defeated sigh. Even she could recognize a losing battle when she saw one. "One word. Real easy."

Time. Another word. One she'd apparently exhausted.

He took hold of her hand before she could turn to leave. "No. Emily, wait."

The quiet, calm of his voice alerted her, followed by an unmistakable sense of foreboding that had nothing to do with their future, or lack of one. "What is it? What's happened?"

"That was Ben. Your grandmother and her nurse are safe, but the school is on fire." He tugged her hand and pulled her close. Blessed numbness finally settled over her, accompanied by a dull buzzing in her ears.

"Baby, I'm sorry," he said. "There's no saving it this time."

DREW SLOWLY DROVE his SUV toward the parking lot across the street from what had once been the Norris Culinary Academy. Huge red trucks lined the boulevard amid trails of snaking hose as firefighters waged a determined battle against the beast.

"Oh my God." Emily's strained whisper pretty much summed up his own feelings.

Thick black smoke billowed from the structure, now completely consumed by flames. The building would be a total loss. All anyone could hope for at this point was to prevent the fire from spreading to neighboring structures.

"How could someone do something like this intentionally?" she asked him. "It doesn't make sense to me."

"An arsonist operates under his own logic. In revenge fires, he twists the truth to suit his own ends to justify his actions." Drew parked at the far end of the lot, away from the hot zone, and killed the engine. "In his mind, he's righting a perceived wrong. An eye for an eye."

Emily unbuckled her seatbelt, then turned to face him. Disbelief added to the worry in her eyes. "Revenge? Are you sure?"

He didn't know why she was surprised when they'd discussed the possibility of revenge previously. "These fires have been intentional and specific," he said. "Like your grandmother said, someone has a match to strike."

Her hands trembled as she opened the door and slid

from the vehicle. "I'm taking my grandmother to a hotel."

"Something you should've done long before now." Fear for what could have happened added to the harsh, reprimanding tone of his voice. "Structures can be replaced. People can't."

She gave him a heated look, then slammed the door. He smacked his hand against the steering wheel in frustration. His day had gone from bad to worse to rotten in less than two hours time. He hated himself for hurting her, but he wasn't exactly thrilled with her at the moment, either. She'd practically rammed his explanation right back down his throat with her half-baked psychoanalysis.

Or had she spoken the truth? Either way, the taste was damned bitter.

"Don't you dare lecture me, Drew," she snapped at him when he caught up with her. "Just catch the bastard so my grandmother can live without fearing some whack job is going to torch what little she has left."

She stalked away from him, heading across the parking lot to where her grandmother watched the devastation from a wheelchair beneath the shade of a jacaranda tree. Suzette stood by her side.

His job began the minute he'd flashed his ID to the uniformed cops at the barricade. Until he received the all clear that it was safe for him to inspect the burn, he had witnesses to interview.

He followed Emily. By the time he reached the trio of women, she had her arms wrapped consolingly around her grandmother's slender shoulders.

"I'm so sorry, Velma," he said when Emily straightened. Emily moved to the opposite side of the wheelchair, ignoring him. The set of her shoulders and defiant tilt of her chin spoke volumes—he'd gone and ticked her off again.

"Thank you," Velma said. She took hold of his hand, her grip surprisingly strong for a woman her age. "I just can't believe it's all gone. Decades. Gone. Did Emily tell you I started the school when my husband was off fighting in the war?"

He crouched beside her, but pale-blue eyes held a faraway look. She'd slipped into the past, into a long-ago era. "With Herbert away, it was up to me to take care of our children. Money was in such short supply, and women of my generation had little experience working outside the home. I could've gotten a job in the old factories, but I had no one to look after my children.

"About all I really did well was cook, so to make ends meet, I offered cooking classes inside our little apartment a couple of nights a week. Most of my students were new brides or young single women hoping to find their way into a man's heart through his stomach. I didn't bother to remind them that most of the men were overseas." A distant smile tipped her lips. "In less than a year I had more students than I could handle by myself.

"When Herb returned from the war," she continued, "with the money I'd saved and the discharge bonus he'd received, we had enough for a down payment on this old two-story building. Ten thousand dollars for real estate back then was a great deal of money. You'd have thought we'd just purchased the Hearst Castle."

Drew blew out a low whistle after mentally estimating the current value of the property. "You'll get a lot more for it now."

"What's left of it," Velma scoffed. She pointed toward the second level, fully engulfed in flames. "We moved our little family upstairs and Herb turned the downstairs into classrooms. After a couple of years, we outgrew the apartment, but we had enough money to build the house. I've lived there for the last fifty years." She let out a sigh. "And now it's gone."

"You still have the house," Emily reassured her.

He didn't argue. From his vantage point, he suspected the burn had been contained. He also knew from his own days on the line before moving into arson, the crew would do everything in their power to save the other structures from damage. But a fire was as unpredictable as a woman, and her mood could change just as swiftly, often with disastrous results.

"You can always rebuild," he told Velma. "The important thing here is that no one's been injured."

Emily tipped her head downward to look at him over the rim of her sunglasses and glared.

He opted to ignore her. For the time being. "Do you know what happened?" he asked Velma. "Did you see anyone or anything suspicious?"

"No. Nothing." She let go of his hand. "I told the officers already that Suzette smelled smoke and called the fire department. Then we left the house and came here to wait."

He stood and focused his attention on Velma's nurse. "Velma said you smelled smoke?"

"Yes," the middle-aged woman offered. "We were just sitting down to breakfast."

"And you didn't hear or see anything?" he questioned, although he already suspected her answer. "No one lurking around the premises?"

"No," Suzette said. "Nothing. I'm sorry. I wish I could be of more help."

"You've done more than enough," Emily said to the nurse after tossing another scathing glance in his direction. "I'm grateful you were here."

"Velma! Velma!"

He looked beyond Suzette's shoulder to see Margo rushing toward them.

"Oh, Velma. This is terrible." Her gravelly voice was strangely breathless. "I was driving by and saw all the smoke. Are you all right?"

Drew frowned. The only reason he and Emily had gotten through the barricades had been because he'd flashed his credentials at the cops who'd cordoned off the area. He scanned the area, but didn't see Margo's blue sedan parked nearby.

"What are you doing here?" Velma asked Margo.

"I was on my way to my daughter's to see her new house," Margo said, her gaze darting rapidly among the group. "And to help her unpack."

Drew tensed, fully alert. From the employment records he'd reviewed, Margo lived approximately twenty miles west of the school. He'd overheard her mention her daughter to Rita, but unless she had more than one daughter who'd recently purchased a home, she should be on her way to Oxnard, which was farther up the coast, and *west* of her own residence, not east near the school.

Margo stared at the structure fire, transfixed. "Oh, this is bad," she murmured. "This is very bad."

Emily removed her sunglasses, cast a meaningful glance in Drew's direction, then shifted her full attention to Margo. "I suppose it's a good thing Grandy didn't agree to partner with you." She spoke slowly, as if choosing her words carefully. "There'll be nothing left of it soon."

Margo remained mesmerized by the fire, fully contained now, as if she hadn't heard Emily.

But Drew had heard every word and understood her meaning perfectly...their firebug had motive. The first place to look for a suspect is *always* in the crowd watching the blaze. By the time he'd arrived at the scene of the previous incidents, no one other than Velma had been present.

Anger filled him, but he tamped down the emotion. He gave Emily a brisk nod so she'd know he'd understood, then took advantage of Margo's distraction with the fire to move far enough away to use his cell phone without being overheard. Within moments, a pair of uniformed patrolmen were walking in their direction.

The minute Margo sensed the officers' presence, she started wringing her hands, but like any garden-variety pyro, her gaze remained transfixed on her work.

Drew moved in behind Margo. The cops flanked her.

"What's going on?" Velma asked, looking from Drew to the cops then finally to Margo, who'd been in her employ for so many years.

"Ma'am," Sean Callahan, a rookie cop Drew had worked with recently on another case, said to Margo. "We'd like to ask you a few questions."

"Margo? Oh, Margo," Velma said, a wealth of sadness entering her gaze. "What have you done?"

Margo kept wringing her hands. "I didn't mean for this to happen. It was an accident. I thought it'd be caught in time, just like all the others."

From her wheelchair, Velma stared up at Margo's stricken face. "Why?" she implored. "Tell me why you would do this to me?"

"I wanted you to sell, Velma. And you kept refusing. I thought if the school became too much of a burden for you, you'd want to be rid of it. I didn't mean for this to happen," Margo repeated.

Callahan led Margo away as his partner read her her rights. She never stopped her repeated babbling, ignoring her right to remain silent.

Drew crouched in front of Velma again. She looked as stricken as Margo had been, but for much more heartbreaking reasons. "Will you be all right?" he asked her.

She gave him a wry little smile, though tears moistened her eyes. "I'm going to be just fine. I've survived a lot during my years, and I'll get through this, too."

He admired this woman's spirit, and could easily see where Emily had gotten her spunk and drive.

"Emily's going to take you to a hotel for a couple of nights until we clean up the area. I have to go now, but when I'm finished, I promise to let you know what's going to happen to Margo."

"Thank you," she said. "I appreciate that."

His gaze caught Emily's as he stood. "Where will you be staying?"

"There's a hotel not far from here."

"I'll call you later."

She removed her sunglasses, revealing her grim expression. "The only thing we have left to say to each other is goodbye."

The word lodged in his throat. Hadn't he been the one who said he didn't want her love? So why was he hesitating?

Eventually, he turned and walked toward his SUV. Goodbye. One word. Not "real easy" as she'd claimed, but *impossible*.

13

ALMOST TWO WEEKS after the fire, Emily was as close to exhaustion as she'd ever come. With her back braced against the porch railing, she sipped from a tall glass of lemonade and watched as the big yellow bulldozer finished off what the fire had left behind, determined to enjoy a moment to herself with nothing more important to occupy her than her drink and the cool sea breeze ruffling the palms and eucalyptus trees.

Two days after the incident, she and her grandmother had moved back into the house, which had gone a long way toward making life somewhat more simple. Since then, her time had been filled with constant meetings and an unprecedented volume of telephone calls with insurance personnel, various contractors, members of the legal profession, architects and builders, plus her own meetings with the creative director of the ad agency to discuss her first assignment. Somehow in all the flurry of activity, she'd managed to put together a solid advertising plan for a local chain of neighborhood restaurants which had thrilled the agency and the client. Not only had she left with notes for two more ad campaigns tucked inside her new briefcase, she'd also received an offer for a full-time position.

Declining the job offer hadn't been easy for someone constantly striving for solidity and security in her life. Neither was starting a new business, but since she'd made the decision to open her own advertising firm she couldn't very well accept the job.

Their first night in the hotel, her grandmother had attempted to convince Emily to run the school if she rebuilt. When Emily had made an off-the-cuff remark about taking over if her grandmother had been running an advertising firm instead of a culinary academy, a very serious, life-altering discussion followed. Emily was still reeling from the combination of making such a monumental decision and a high like none she'd ever known at the prospect of becoming wholly self-sufficient.

The property would be rebuilt, but as standard office space rather than a culinary academy. Instead of offering her a start-up loan, Grandy would be her silent partner in a new business venture—Dugan Advertising. Emily's agency would occupy the bottom floor, leaving the upper level available to rent.

No wonder she was exhausted, she thought as the gentle afternoon breeze cooled her skin. The week had been a nonstop whirlwind of activity with little sleep to recharge her rapidly dwindling batteries. She couldn't place blame entirely on the series of meetings and endless phone calls. Each night she fell into bed exhausted, only to toss and turn. When sleep eventually claimed her, dreams haunted her until the alarm rang a few hours later, leaving her achy and empty.

She missed Drew. She missed him so much it hurt to

breathe if she allowed herself to think about him for any length of time. Ignoring the pain inside was next to impossible. Each passing day brought not relief but an amplification of the emptiness.

As he'd promised her grandmother, Drew had indeed come to the hotel following Margo's questioning at police headquarters. When he'd called from the hotel lobby, she'd answered the phone, given him the room number, then promptly disappeared, escaping like a coward because she couldn't face him. Knowing she'd never again feel the strength of his arms around her, never feel the weight of his finely tuned body over hers, or hear the deep, soothing sound of his voice or the joy of his laughter, had been too much for her to bear.

She'd returned to the hotel after a long walk along the shore, making certain his SUV was gone before going back to the room. Her grandmother had been suspiciously silent about her behavior, but at least hadn't battered her with questions or sagacious advice.

She hadn't heard from Drew since. She'd expected she'd have to deal with him eventually with regard to the arson investigation, but he'd solved the potentially uncomfortable situation by turning the remainder of the case over to Dave Byrd.

Once again, he'd made his position painfully clear.

She forced the lump threatening to lodge in her throat down with a big swallow of lemonade, but the cool liquid botched the job by failing to alleviate the tears clouding her vision.

She let out a weighty sigh and checked her wristwatch. She needed to shower and change for dinner. Grandy and her nurse would be returning from the physical therapy session for her injured arm and hand soon, and Emily had promised her grandmother a nice evening out at the Santa Monica Pier.

She reached for the railing, but her hand stilled in midair when she spotted a white luxury sedan pulling into the lot and parking amid the vehicles of the debris-removal crew. The door opened and the driver stepped out of the car, shielding his eyes from the bright California sunshine. He spied her and waved, then headed straight for her.

She blinked, once, twice, three times, certain her eyesight was failing her. "What are you doing here, Charlie?" she asked when he reached the brick steps. Although her anger with him had faded days ago, she'd certainly barked the question at him. Not her fault, she reasoned. His presence shocked her clear down to her sandals.

Charles Pruitt, III, shrugged his slender shoulders. "I thought we should talk."

She set down the empty glass of lemonade, then wrapped her arms around her shins. "Long distance would've been cheaper."

A half smile curved his thin lips. "You're going to make this difficult for me, aren't you?"

She let out a sigh and patted the space next to her on the porch. "It seems to be my specialty lately."

"You look good, Emily," he said as he sat, then smoothed the sharp-pressed seams of his suit trousers.

No, she didn't, but she appreciated the lie just the

same. Little sleep and constant running from one meeting to the next, plus nursing a broken heart had left her wrung out and lethargic. The faded navy plaid seersucker capris and loose-fitting white tank top she'd changed into after another exhausting day hardly dispelled the image, but she'd been aiming for comfort.

"So do you," she told him without fibbing. Unlike her, Charlie didn't know how to look like something a cat hid beneath the dirt in the flower garden. For as long as she'd known him, he'd always looked his best, neatly pressed, clean-shaven and not a single blond hair out of place. What he lacked in people skills, he made up for in physical presence.

He swiped a nonexistent speck of dust from his wing tips, then smoothed his perfectly straight yellow-and-navy power tie. "I behaved badly the last time we spoke."

An understatement, in her opinion. "Yeah, you did," she agreed. The sting of resentment zapped her at the reminder of his less-than-supportive response to the news she was having a baby. *His* baby.

He cleared his throat, but kept his gaze on the workmen. "I am sorry about that. You…uh…took me a little by surprise with your news."

"So I gathered." She leaned back on her hands and stretched her legs over the steps. "Why are you here, Charlie?"

"You. The baby."

Her brows winged up. After their last phone call, she'd been under the distinct impression she and the baby weren't of much importance to him. "Then I suggest you take the next flight back to New York," she said none too charitably. "*My* baby and I are just fine, thank you very much."

Charlie stayed silent, his expression thoughtful. If he believed for a second he could convince her to return to New York with him, then he was in for yet another surprise. Forget that he'd cheated on her or that she'd never be able to trust him again. The truth was much more simple—she hadn't loved Charlie. Oh, she'd cared about him, and his infidelity had definitely hurt—her pride, not her heart. As she'd told Drew, no one could damage what hadn't belonged to them in the first place. That privilege belonged solely to Drew.

Finally, Charlie cast his golden-brown eyes her way, his patrician features contemplative. "You're really not coming back, are you?" he asked. "To New York, I mean."

Relief filled her. She lacked the energy to engage in another relationship postmortem. They were losing battles she no longer had a desire to wage. "No, Charlie. I told you two weeks ago, my life is here now."

He pursed his thin lips. "That will complicate matters."

She frowned. "Meaning…"

"Meaning, how are we going to handle this?"

"What do you mean *we*?" There was no *we* as far as she and Charlie were concerned.

"I meant about the baby."

She turned her head to watch the workmen clear away more rubble. "Like I said, *we* aren't going to do anything."

"I always thought you'd make a good lawyer. You're so argumentative, Emily." He let out a sigh filled with defeat. "It's frustrating, especially when I came to see you so we could reach an amicable resolution to our little problem."

"Oh, for freaking Pete's sake, Charlie." She rolled her eyes before looking at him again. "Our little *problem?* What century did you drop out of?"

"I really don't want to fight with you." His voice didn't rise, although she did detect a slight hint of annoyance. His cool demeanor never showed an ounce of emotion. In fact, now that she thought about it, the only time she could remember Charlie ever losing his cool had been during their telephone conversation that day she told him the news. He lacked...passion, she decided, a character flaw she held in overwhelming supply.

"Then what do you want?" she asked irritably. "You have a tidy little legal document tucked inside your blazer pocket for me to sign that says I and *my* baby will never darken your doorstep?"

"No," he said, giving her his full attention. "That won't be necessary. But you should know, I don't think I'm ready to be a parent."

"And you think I am?" A bubble of laughter erupted. "If people actually waited until they were ready to have children, Charlie, the human race would cease to exist."

"Yes, but the difference is I don't *want* to be a father." He let out a hefty sigh. "Emily, children frighten me."

His honesty surprised her, leaving her momentarily speechless.

"Financially, I'll uphold my responsibility," he continued, "but I won't fight you for joint custody or visitation."

No one had ever called her a Pollyanna, but in the last two weeks, she'd swear her sunglasses had taken on a rose-colored tint when she hadn't been looking. "You're serious?"

He offered her a solemn nod. "I've had time to think about it. I do want what's best for the baby." He looked down, then swiped at more nonexistent dust. "And for you," he added as an afterthought.

She digested his words, truly stunned by his statement. "Charlie, do you realize what you're saying?" she asked after a moment. "Do you understand what it is you're so willing to give up?"

When he finally looked over at her again, his brows were knitted with obvious confusion. "Honestly? No," he admitted sheepishly. "Does that upset you?"

"It surprises me," she told him, not quite certain what he expected of her. To give him an out? Let him off the hook?

"Since we're being honest," she said carefully, "I'm not sure if you view this baby as an inconvenience, with distaste or if you're just apathetic."

"Confusion," he admitted. After a moment's pause, he shrugged. "I don't know how I'm supposed to feel. Maybe if we were still a couple, I'd feel differently about it."

Whether or not they were a couple made no difference to her whatsoever. A baby was involved, and regardless of the circumstances, such a priceless gift was worthy of a celebration of joy. Something she wasn't sure ol' Cheatin' Charlie completely comprehended.

Her options were clear—either plant her sandal on his backside and give him a hard shove out of her and the baby's life once and for all, or they could attempt to reach an amicable solution. He *was* the father, after all, and that provided him with certain rights, both legal and moral. She'd never deny him his child, but she did have one caveat.

"I'm not going to prevent you from being a part of the baby's life," she said. "But I'm not going to force you to be an active parent, either. That's something you have to decide for yourself. All I ask is that if you do participate, it can't be only when it's convenient. This is a full-time job, even with our geography issues."

He definitely looked spooked. "But how? It's not going to be easy with you living here and me in New York."

She pulled her legs up again, folded her arms and rested them on her knees. "We can figure out the geography later. But—" she paused until she had his full attention "—I do want an answer now, Charlie. Will you or will you not be a father to this baby?"

His Adam's apple bobbed up and down. "I'm willing to try if you are." The words erupted in a rush, followed by another hefty sigh. "Yes," he said, more firmly. "I want to do this, Emily."

She smiled at him. "Was it really that difficult?"

His expression turned sheepish and he nodded. "Do you hate me for it?"

"I don't hate you," she said and realized she meant every word. "What you did to me was sleazy, yes, but I think we both know now that we weren't right for each other. If we had been, you never would've found someone else." And she never would have fallen so hard and fast for Drew, she thought sadly.

He reached for her hand, brought it to his mouth and lightly brushed his lips over her knuckles. "You're an incredible woman, Emily Dugan. Argumentative, but still pretty incredible. I have a feeling you're not going to have any trouble finding the guy that's right for you some day."

Little did he know, she already had found him. Too bad he didn't want her, too.

THE FIRST ALARM had sounded less than ten minutes after Drew walked through the bay at Trinity Station on Thursday morning. Within the hour, three more alarms had been struck, bringing a total of seven engine crews, two ladder crews and one rescue to fight the largest blaze in Santa Monica history.

A total of fifty-seven firefighters had been called in to battle the flaming beast. Fourteen homes and acres of hillside had been claimed. Initial property-damage estimates of the prime real estate skyrocketed into the millions. New homes would eventually replace those destroyed. New saplings and plant life would slowly restore the charred acres of hillside.

Nothing could restore the life of their fallen brother.

Amid the squawk of radios and the redundant flash of spinning lights atop the engines as the crews rolled up, an eerie hush permeated the area. Every member of the department felt the loss. They didn't have to work beside Ivan "Fitz" Fitzpatrick on a daily basis, or even know him personally. No man or woman wearing the uniform was immune to the myriad of emotions when one of their own was lost. The stress team would be called for a debriefing, but nothing could completely alleviate the sometimes dangerous combination of guilt and relief that easily reached clear to the bottom of the soul.

Drew understood the guilt of survival. Even the morbid sense of relief they all silently shared made sense to him. Unlike Fitz, he and the other members had been spared. It was the harboring of relief that was especially difficult and brought with it an even deeper sense of shame.

Drew looked up from the notes he'd taken after interviewing several more witnesses. Grime and soot covered Ben's face and gear. Pain lined his brother's face, but Drew suspected Ben's pain ran deeper than most today.

As Incident Commander, Ben had been the one to send Fitz into a residence to perform a search-and-rescue operation for two small children and their young mother trapped on the second story. After safely handing the children through a window to the waiting ladder team, he'd gone back to search for the children's mother.

As the lead investigator on scene, Drew had been interviewing witnesses to the initial flames when he'd spotted heavy fire venting from the roof. He'd immediately reported the news to Ben. The structural integrity of the house had been compromised, and despite Ben's order for a series of short horn blasts to signal immediate evacuation, Fitz never made it out. The young mother had miraculously been spared, but last thing they'd heard had been a brief radio call for help seconds before the roof collapsed. Fitz was trapped and running out of air.

Ben jerked off his helmet, his expression grim. "I told Cap we'd go see Krista. I figured you'd want to be there, too."

"Of course," Drew said without hesitation.

Drew and Fitz had started at Trinity Station at the same time. All the crew members shared that same unique bond so common among those who routinely put their lives on the line, but coming up together had made his bond with Fitz tighter. When Drew had been accepted onto the arson squad, Fitz had thrown a party to celebrate. An event, Drew realized suddenly, that had taken place a mere few blocks from Emily's grandmother's place.

A fresh stab of guilt pierced his already battered conscience, but in no way garnered enough power to alter his decision regarding his affair with Emily, any more than her arguments had done. Cutting his losses sooner rather than later hadn't stopped him from thinking about her, though.

Or wanting her.

Or, dammit, loving her.

"How much longer you got?" Ben asked him, inclining his head toward the paperwork in Drew's hands.

"About half an hour. Meet you back at the station house?"

Ben nodded and turned to go.

"Hey!" Drew called to his brother.

Ben stopped to look over his shoulder.

"It wasn't your fault," Drew told him. "It was an accident."

Ben turned away and walked silently toward the engine. He didn't have to say anything. Drew easily read the deep pain underscoring his oldest brother's eyes and knew Ben didn't believe him for a second.

14

A THICK, palpable silence accompanied Drew and Ben on the drive to the Fitzpatrick home, each of them lost in their own tortuous thoughts of the dreadful task ahead. The spouse of every firefighter, cop, even airline pilots knew of the dangers of the job, but the knowledge did nothing to avert Drew's discomfort. Nor had the words of their captain as they'd left the firehouse, that Krista Fitzpatrick was a strong woman, a good wife and she'd survive the devastating loss. She had no choice, the captain had said. She had two sons depending on her, now more than ever.

Drew knew from his own experience that wasn't always the case.

He thought of Emily and her brutal assault on his beliefs. No, he thought suddenly. She'd brutally assaulted the truth, forcing him to examine the past from her eyes.

None of it mattered. Not in the long run, because nothing had changed and never would for one simple reason, the past couldn't be altered. History could not be rewritten.

The task that lay ahead only served to cement more firmly in his mind that he'd made the right decision ending their relationship, a decision that had nothing to do with her ridiculous claim, grossly lacking in foundation. He was not afraid of being alone.

Ben parked at the curb in front of a modest suburban tract home. Drew's apprehension grew when Ben killed the engine and dragged his keys from the ignition. He'd never had to make a visit like the one he and Ben were about to, but he had a pretty good idea of what to expect. Many of his memories of that horrible night had faded with time, but he'd never forget the sight of Ben attempting to comfort their inconsolable father, never forget how frightened he'd been as his father's rage had flown out of control. He'd never forget how, in his rage, his father had lashed out at them verbally, laying the blame for their mother giving up the fight to live at their feet.

Joanna Perry had waited three long days to die. She'd waited until she'd been able to say goodbye.

"Do you want to wait here?" Ben asked him.

"No," he said. "I owe it to Fitz."

He understood Ben's concern, knew his overprotective nature made him ask the question. Since that horrible night so many years ago, Ben had done everything in his power to shield him and Cale from life's harsh realities. Reality didn't get much harsher than telling a wife her husband had been lost in the line of duty.

Together they left the quiet of Ben's pickup truck and walked quietly up the concrete walkway to the front door of the Fitzpatrick home. Drew hung back, waiting for Krista to answer once Ben rang the doorbell.

Ben reached for the bell a second time just as the front door swung open. A heartbeat later, the purpose of their visit dawned, flooding Krista Fitzpatrick's almond-colored eyes with heavy moisture. Her thick, black hair made her appear even more frighteningly pale as the blood drained from her face. She held the edge of the door with her hand, her knuckles turning white from the force of her grip. "Oh God," she whispered, shaking her head from side to side. "No. No."

Ben caught Krista as her knees gave out on her. As if she were as fragile as china, he gently held her close to his side and guided her back into the house, to the family room and onto the brown L-shaped corduroy sofa.

Helplessness swamped Drew as the force of Krista's sobs wracked her small body. He didn't know what he was supposed to do. There were no words he could offer to alleviate the horrendous shock or acute heartache. Nothing but meaningless platitudes.

The television blared as a local news station broadcast the events of the day. A steady red bar filled the very bottom of the screen, proclaiming two fatalities. A news chopper circled the area, providing viewers an aerial perspective of the destruction, courtesy a gas leak that had gone undetected. Apparently the leak had been in the gas line to a clothes dryer. When the home owner turned on the dryer, the force of the explosion had literally blown the roof off the place. By the time the first engine crew arrived on scene, the fire had already spread.

Drew scooped the remote from the coffee table and turned off the television, then took off down the hall to the bathroom and returned with a box of tissues. "I'm so sorry," he said softly, as he sat on the short end of the sofa to face Krista and Ben.

She stared at her hands, twisting her diamond wedding ring around and around on her finger. When she looked up at them, her eyes, usually filled with laughter, were rimmed in red. "How?" she finally asked, reaching for a tissue.

Ben glossed over much of the details as best he could. "The roof collapsed," he finished. "There wasn't anything anyone could do."

"It's been all over the news," she told them. "They said there'd been two fatalities and one critical. They released the name of the patient and the woman who'd died, but not... When they wouldn't say whether or not the other fatality had been a firefighter, I knew. I prayed it wasn't..." Fresh tears spilled from her eyes. "I prayed it wasn't anyone we knew. You know they won't release the name until the next of kin had been notified, but you wait anyway, hoping to hear a name so you know it's not you they're waiting to notify."

"Krista, what can we do for you?" Drew asked her. "Just name it."

A tentative smile touched her lips. "Bring Fitz home," she whispered, fighting back another onslaught of tears.

A lump the size of Chicago lodged in his throat.

She let out a deep shuddering breath. "You know, you try not to think about what could happen. You wake up in the morning, you kiss your husband goodbye and only allow yourself one very brief moment of panic as he walks out the door. It's all you're allowed, because you can't live your life in a constant state of fear. So you end up fooling yourself into believing it'll never be you that has to hear those two horrible useless words, 'I'm sorry.' You know it's all a lie anyway, the make-believe. But that lie makes the waiting for him to come home again bearable because the alternative is unimaginable."

She offered them a weak smile. "But the unthinkable has happened, and I can't stop thinking that this is the way Fitz would have wanted to go. Fighting fires. Saving lives. God, he loved it. A firefighter is who he was, and even now, even right this second, I wouldn't have changed that about him even if I could."

"I know it's hard." Ben's voice was suspiciously strained. "You're not alone. Don't forget that."

Drew cleared his throat. "He didn't suffer," he told her, because it was the right thing to say. "I hope that gives you at least some comfort."

"It'll be a while before I'm comforted about anything, but thank you. I appreciate you telling me. It'll help, eventually."

"Is there someone we can call for you?" Ben asked.

She shook her head. "No. I'll call Fitz's parents a little later. They'll need to make arrangements to fly out for the..." Her voice trailed off, and she clamped her hand over her mouth, unable, or unwilling to utter that final word.

Drew handed her another tissue. "You shouldn't be alone tonight. Why don't you let us call your folks or your sister to come stay with you."

"No," she said, her voice firm. "I'll be fine. I've got the boys and I need to be strong for them. They need me, now more than ever. Besides," she added with another hint of a wavering smile, "Fitz would never forgive me if I fell apart on them."

Drawing his next breath took effort on Drew's part. Krista's inner strength, her determination to hold it all together for the sake of her children during the most devastating event of her life sliced through nearly a quarter century of conviction. It cut apart a belief system he'd harbored and nursed and fed with care, allowing it to skew his reality until he knew nothing else.

The pain of loss was indeed devastating, he'd lived through it not once, but twice, and he'd made it his mission in life to avoid that kind of pain again at all costs. Tilly had accused him of intentionally dating women who were wrong for him. Emily accused him of some twisted form of commitment atheism.

They were right. He avoided not only commitment, but anything that even remotely resembled the concept. But the truth, the deep-seated cause, had nothing whatsoever to do with his fear of putting another through the pain of loss. It was all about his own fears of being swallowed and consumed by the incredible darkness himself.

Krista drew in a sharp breath. "Oh God," she said. "How do I tell the boys? They'll be home from school any minute."

Drew reached across the small space separating them and took hold of Krista's hands. "You tell them their dad was a hero," he said. "And how much he loved them."

Words his own father had never stepped out of his own self-pity long enough to tell his own sons. Instead, he'd cast useless blame where it hadn't been deserved and had embarked upon a selfish journey of self-destruction. Alex Perry hadn't kept his wife's memory alive, but had single-handedly destroyed everything she'd ever stood for or believed in—duty, honor and most importantly, the unconditional love of her children.

By the time they left, Drew understood with acute clarity that he needed to make a drastic change in his life, or, as Emily predicted, he'd end up a lonely old man—just like his father. And that, he decided, was not something he would allow to happen.

Ben followed Drew out onto the stoop, then pulled a white business card from his pocket and handed it to Krista. "For when you're ready."

"What's this?" she asked.

A big yellow school bus pulled up a few doors down. The doors creaked open, following by the shouts and laughter of several children as they exited the bus.

"A support group," Ben told her. "For surviving families of fallen firefighters."

"Are you sure you don't want us to stay?" Drew asked.

Krista tucked the card in the back pocket of her jeans. "Thanks, but no. Don't worry," she said, then laid her hand on Ben's arm. "We really will be okay."

Drew and Ben left. As they slipped inside Ben's truck, Fitz's dark-haired sons raced across the lawn to their mom. Drew buckled his seatbelt watching closely.

Krista greeted her boys and hugged them close, then led them into the house. Not once did she allow them to see an ounce of the deep sadness inside her.

EMILY RIPPED the yellow sheet of paper from the legal pad, balled it up and chucked it halfway across the kitchen into the garbage can to join her four other less-than-brilliant ideas for the hair color ad campaign. From her chair at the table she caught glimpses of the television sitcom her grandmother and Suzette were watching. She noted thankfully that there were no further news alerts recapping the hillside fire that morning.

She'd started worrying about Drew the minute she'd heard the first media report on the radio while she sat in traffic on the Santa Ana Freeway. She had no idea whether he, his brother or any of the other members of Trinity Station she'd met the night of Cale and Amanda's wedding were involved in fighting the fire, but that didn't stop her from racing to the car once her meeting with the architect and builder drew to a close three hours later for more news.

The announcement of two fatalities at the scene of the fire increased her worry to near panic when the press didn't release any names. She attempted to reason with herself that Drew was probably safe, and repeated those words over and over in her mind like a mantra.

Her grandmother and Suzette were practically glued to the television by the time she reached the house after more seemingly endless errands. If they hadn't released a name by the time of the six o'clock newscast, she'd been prepared to call the firehouse herself and demand to know if Drew was safe. Only it hadn't been necessary. As they flashed a photograph of Ivan Fitzpatrick on the screen, she silently prayed for his wife and children.

She'd only met Fitz and his wife briefly, but she still ached—for Krista and her children, but especially for Drew. Loss was not something he suffered well, and although she understood she wasn't doing herself any favors by worrying about him, she couldn't help herself. The man had insinuated himself into her heart. He'd taken up residence in her soul and to her knowledge, no legal notice to quit existed for that kind of eviction.

She tapped the legal pad with the tip of her pen, forcing herself to concentrate on hair color rather than imaginary eviction notices.

When the tapping failed to spark an idea, she stared at the blank page as her grandmother and Suzette laughed at the antics of some sitcom couple. The client wanted hip and fresh. Hips were plentiful, courtesy of the changes already occurring within her body. The blank page mocked her. Apparently fresh was sold out.

Females had been waging a war against the aging

process for centuries, and advertisers encouraged the fight with a bombardment of new and improved weapons on a daily basis. The advertising industry had already ordered women to wash the gray out of their hair, promised that blondes would have more fun, and spent billions of client dollars reminding them they're worth it or they weren't getting older, only better. The target audience had been sold on the concept of renewing and reconditioning, vitalizing and nourishing their hair color, rather than their souls.

Her eyebrows winged upward as inspiration struck. Time slipped away as she made notes about vitalizing the inner self and taking charge of destinies with a new look, inside and out. When she eventually ran out of steam, she had enough notes to create an entire series of ads for the client's campaign.

Satisfied, she cleared away her notes and the few hasty sketches she'd made, then walked into the living room. Too bad her broken heart couldn't be cured with something as simple as a change in hair color, she thought.

Her grandmother dozed while Suzette crocheted and watched a medical drama simultaneously. "I'm going to get some air," Emily whispered to Suzette, then quietly opened the front door.

She squeaked with fright, startled to find a dark shadowy figure on the other side of the screen. She flipped on the porch light. Drew. "What are you doing here?"

"We need to talk."

The velvet-smooth quality of his deep voice awoke

every cell in her body. She'd managed to take a few giant steps since she'd last seen him—her life, her career were on a steady path and gaining ground daily. The sight of him, even through the screen, reminded her that her heart hadn't gained so much as a single baby step toward healing.

Wasn't it enough that she thought about him constantly? Did he have to show up on her doorstep and remind her of what they could never have together?

"What is it?" her grandmother asked from the sofa, now fully awake. "Who's there?"

"It's okay, Grandy," she said, keeping the flimsy barrier of the screen door between her and Drew. "I was startled by a rat lurking at the door."

Under the buttery glow of the porch light, Drew winced. "You're going to make this difficult, aren't you?"

"Why does everyone keep asking me that question?"

"Because you're habitually contrary," her grandmother muttered just loud enough for her to hear.

"What if I don't want to talk to you?"

"Then don't. You can listen while I talk." He opened the door, snagged her hand and tugged her out onto the porch with him.

His touch set off a series of sparks zipping over her skin in all directions. What had she been thinking? Baby steps? Crawling would be a vast improvement, and he'd just set her progress back with one rather impersonal touch.

To maintain her tenuous grip on her sanity and to

keep her hormones from zinging off the charts, she tugged her hand free of his and moved to the far edge of the porch. With her backside parked against the railing, she crossed her arms and refused to look at him. "Fine," she said, "Talk. But if you've come here to put a matching Nike imprint on my other cheek, forget it."

"What are you talking about?" He sounded thoroughly confused.

She let out a sigh, not bothering to explain. "You had something to say?"

Say you've been a big, stupid jerk and that you're not good enough for me to love. Say your life is empty without me.

And then what? Was she supposed to forgive him for breaking her heart? Surely he didn't expect her to run back into his arms, thanking the deity in charge of love for such a gracious gift, as if he hadn't trampled her heart.

Was she supposed to trust him not to hurt her again?

I don't think so.

Say it, you big stupid jerk, and I'll think about it.

Her ire died when he closed the distance between them and she had her first good look at him. *Haggard* barely scratched the surface. The dancing light in his incredible green eyes had vanished. No sign of the playful smile usually curving his kissable mouth existed, reminding her of what he must be feeling at the loss of his friend.

"I heard about Fitz," she said. "I'm so sorry."

He stuffed his hands in the pockets of his trousers and looked down at the ground between their feet. "Thank you," he said. "It's been a rough day."

He told her about the fire and the accident that had taken Fitz, about the heartbreaking visit he and Ben had made to tell Krista her husband wouldn't be coming home tonight. She listened, heard the pain in his voice, saw the emotion brightening his eyes and the final barricade surrounding her battered heart and supporting her wounded pride crumbled into a pile of rubble.

He held her gaze. "I was wrong, Emily."

"About?"

"Everything," he admitted.

"Oh really?" she said, determined to protect herself from more pain now that he'd managed to strip away the last of her defenses. "And what brings you to such an unprecedented conclusion?"

He reached for her, and cupped her cheek in the warmth of his palm. "I've missed you."

Ditto. Ditto. Ditto, her conscience screamed. "I hear cats are great company. You might consider getting one for yourself."

The barest hint of a smile touched his mouth. "You were right," he said, smoothing his thumb along her jaw.

She rolled her eyes. "About?"

"Everything."

She was getting a little tired of his one-word replies. "Specifics, please." Her grandmother was right. She *was* habitually contrary.

"About me being afraid." He dropped his hand and laced his fingers with hers. "I was afraid. I still am because I love you so much it hurts. Here," he said, lifting their joined hands and placing them over his heart. "Loving you scares the hell out of me, but if the alternative is to spend the rest of my life without you, I don't think I can live with that, either."

"You hurt me," she said, reluctant to let him off the hook so easily. He *had* hurt her, but she couldn't deny she loved him with every ounce of her soul. No matter how much she'd wanted to steal it back, she couldn't, because every part of her truly belonged to Drew, a sexy charmer who'd sweet-talked his way past her defenses, made a mockery of her common sense and headed straight for her heart as if it were his right, his own claim to Manifest Destiny.

"I know and I'm sorry." His mouth brushed hers, sweet, kind and so tender she nearly wept.

"Forgive me, Emily, and I'll spend the rest of my life making it up to you. I promise."

Her vocal cords refused to cooperate.

"Say something, sweetheart."

Too choked with emotion to speak, she showed him instead by wrapping her arms around his neck, plastering her body against his and kissing him with all the love in her heart.

"Emily?" Suzette's tentative voice penetrated the heat already simmering inside her. "Velma wants to know if you've forgiven him or if you need Herb's old varmint gun?"

Emily giggled. It'd been a long time since she'd been busted necking with some guy on the porch. But this wasn't just some guy. This was Drew, who made her

hotter than a heatwave and filled her soul with exquisite joy.

"Tell her the varmint's been caged," he called. "And
he couldn't be happier," he finished saying on a whisper for her ears only.

"She's forgiven him," they heard Suzette say as she
closed the front door and turned off the porch light to
give them privacy.

"Now," she said, snuggling closer, "about this making it up to me part..."

He chuckled and zeroed in on the spot just below her
ear. A flash of heat raced down her spine and spread
with languid warmth throughout her body. Her sweet-
talking charmer was definitely off to a very good start.

*   *   *   *   *

Don't miss the third and final story in the
SOME LIKE IT HOT
miniseries by RITA® Award-nominated author
Jamie Denton!

Check out
UNDER FIRE
on sale November 2003
at your favorite retail outlet.

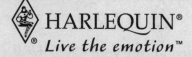

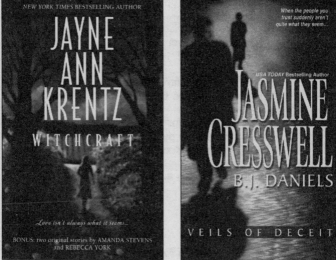

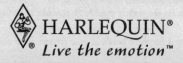

COMING NEXT MONTH

#949 IT'S ALL ABOUT EVE Tracy Kelleher
When tap pants go missing not once, but *three* times, lingerie-store
owner Eve Cantoro calls in the cops. As soon as Carter Moran arrives,
he hopes Eve will keep calling, and often! The chemistry between
them is red-hot, and as events heat up at the shop, Eve's stock isn't
the only lingerie that goes missing....

#950 UNDER FIRE Jamie Denton
Some Like It Hot, Bk. 3
OSHA investigator Jana Linney has never had really *good* sex.
So when she meets sexy firefighter Ben Perry, she decides to do
something about it. Having a one-night stand isn't like her, but if anyone can "help" her, Ben can. Only, one night isn't enough...
and a repeat performance is unlikely, once Jana discovers she's investigating the death of one of Ben's co-workers. Still, now
that Jana's tasted what sex *should* be, she's *not* giving it up....

#951 ONE NAUGHTY NIGHT Joanne Rock
The Wrong Bed—linked to Single in South Beach
Renzo Cesare has always been protective toward women. So it makes
complete sense for him to "save" the beautiful but obviously out of
her league Esmerelda Giles at a local nightclub. But it doesn't make
sense for him to claim to be her blind date. He's not sure where *that*
impulse came from. But before he can figure out a way to tell her the
truth, she's got him in a lip lock so hot, he'll say anything to stay
there!

#952 BARELY BEHAVING Jennifer LaBrecque
Heat
After three dead-end trips down the matrimonial highway,
Tammy Cooper is giving up on marriage. She's the town bad
girl—and she's proud of it. From now on, her motto is "Love 'em
and leave 'em." Only, her plan takes a hit when gorgeous veterinarian
Niall Fortson moves in next door. He's more than willing to let
Tammy love him all she wants. But he's not letting her go any-
where....

HTCNM1003